SISTER OF THE ANGELS

A Christmas Story

ELIZABETH GOUDGE

Girls Gone By Publishers

COMPLETE AND UNABRIDGED

Published by Girls Gone By Publishers
The Vicarage, Church Street, Coleford, Radstock, Somerset, BA3 5NG
www.ggbp.co.uk

First published by Duckworth 1939
First published by Girls Gone By Publishers 2014; new edition 2021
Text © The Estate of Elizabeth Goudge
Christmas Journeys © Mia Jha 2021
A View for First-Time Readers © John Gough 2021
A View for Experienced Goudge Readers © John Gough 2021
Tower House, Wells © Ann Mackie-Hunter; photographs © Vicky Egan
Publishing History © Clarissa Cridland 2014, 2021
Note on the Text © Laura Hicks and Sarah Woodall 2014, 2021
Design and Layout © Girls Gone By Publishers 2021

Neither Girls Gone By Publishers nor any of their authors or
contributors have any responsibility for the continuing accuracy
of URLs for external or third-party websites referred to in this
book; nor do they guarantee that any content on such websites
is, or will remain, accurate or appropriate.

Cover design by Ken Websdale
Typeset in England by GGBP
Printed and bound by Short Run Press, Exeter
ISBN 978-1-84745-301-3

CONTENTS

CHRISTMAS JOURNEYS

Sister of the Angels has a special place on my Christmas reading list each year. It is a delight to reach the title page and read 'A Christmas Story by Elizabeth Goudge', and then to turn to the dedication to know that it is 'for those who love Henrietta'. And who could not? To spend some time during Advent with Henrietta is a welcome delight indeed. First published by Duckworth in 1939 and then by GGBP in 2014, *Sister of the Angels* sits between *A City of Bells* (1936) and *Henrietta's House* (1942) in Elizabeth Goudge's Torminster series of novels featuring the eponymous Henrietta. It is impossible to overshadow Henrietta and her comings and goings, but in *Angels* we find Torminster Cathedral itself taking a central place, pivotal to the plot and bringing a focal point to the Christmas celebrations. The cathedral also provides the backdrop to one of the book's key themes, that of patience and understanding for ourselves and others.

Torminster Cathedral is richly described throughout the book. As a focal point in the city, 'it rose up like some great enchanted mountain' (p74). It is no surprise that visitors throng to see it, even during the Winter months. By Christmas Eve, the cathedral warms to be 'not so much the house of life as the house of comfort inside life' (p140). As in the real world, when sometimes we visit a place that has a profound effect on us, so too visiting Torminster Cathedral transforms characters in unexpected ways. In our current age, when the thought of being a 'tourist' may sound slightly consumeristic, 'visitor' suggests a more meaningful encounter, and 'guest' sounds best of all, suggesting as it does that the eagerness of the visitor will be matched in the welcome they receive. It is, of course, especially pertinent to think of welcoming travellers and guests at Christmas.

This sense of welcoming guests is reflected in one of my favourite passages in *Sister of the Angels*, when Henrietta first meets the stranger at the cathedral: 'She was naturally friendly and Grandfather had trained her to be very courteous to Cathedral visitors, no matter how tiresome they might be. They were the guests of the Cathedral and all possible information and assistance should be offered them' (p80). What I especially love about this passage is the sense of the cathedral as a living place, open to all those who enter. Through Henrietta's characteristic sensitivity, Elizabeth Goudge is able to draw the impact of this 'mysterious great building that man had built to the glory of God' (p76) down to human scale: 'The place in its eternal greatness and grandeur seemed to her as frightening as life itself … Although she was only eleven she knew that some people found life very frightening' (p76). Perhaps all cathedral guests, and maybe especially the tiresome ones, were in need of great courtesy partly so as not to be overawed by the space in which they found themselves. Later, during the Christmas service, the choir sings: '*The hopes and fears of all the years are met in thee to-night*' and proceeds 'down the worn steps; so worn by countless worshippers that they were bent to the shape of a bow as though always weighed down by the feet of the multitude' (p148). Here too, then, Elizabeth Goudge expresses the connection between the human frailty of the people and their literal footprint in their search for the eternal and the divine. There is no need here for distinctions between those of amiable or tiresome dispositions. In this space, all footsteps are welcome.

Whilst we might well wish for ever-amiable travelling companions through life, *Sister of the Angels* provides some considered thoughts on practising patience and tolerance. The gentle way in which Elizabeth Goudge rounds out each character with both failings and nobilities gives ample scope for contemplation (which may prove useful before large family Christmas gatherings). 'Whatever our sins', Grandfather wisely counsels, 'there is good in all' (p88). Henrietta applies a practical lens to that advice, when she reflects that people, even grown-ups, need to allow themselves to be looked after at times. Gabriel's 'genius in escaping responsibility' (p62) is balanced by his wisdom 'when dealing with humanity in distress' (p99). Her adoptive brother's difficult moods and Napoleonic positions might come and go, but 'there were few who were not persuaded to happiness by Hugh Anthony' (p120). Although Henrietta is 'well aware of the sterling goodness that existed under the little old lady's outward asperity' (p100), she does have to count to large numbers (Grandfather's sage advice to control a rising temper) on occasions when Grandmother's asperity is aimed at her father. Henrietta also observes a 'downright greed' (p101) in Grandfather's delight in helping others, although his ceaseless compassion and generosity are always evident. And as for Henrietta herself, it is a Christmas story after all, so whilst she may not have always fully completed her daily ablutions, her 'radiance was as a lamp that is deliberately lit and carried to a place where the shadows are darkest' (p120). It is a story about bringing people together, with wise understanding and making allowance for all. In a time when the furthest we may be able to easily travel is to put ourselves in someone else's shoes, Elizabeth Goudge's beautiful Christmas story reminds us that we come together as a community, with all our failings and nobilities.

As it is a happy Christmas story, it also seems only right to mention a few of the moments in the book that highlight Elizabeth Goudge's great imagination and wit. The book is filled with them, and readers will surely find their own, but some of my favourites include the description of Hugh Anthony's story-telling in which 'ignorance of his subject merely lent wings to his imagination' (p66); the useful advice that 'you must stop to pick up an Archdeacon when you knock him over' (p94); and Martha, that best of gossips, in whose hands 'reputations and characters … were merely enhanced in glory and virtue' (p123). Like Henrietta's pink paper bag filled with satin prauleens, such passages are pure delight. In many ways, this imaginative novella reminds us to be grateful for our fellow travellers this Christmastide.

I do hope you enjoy reading *Sister of the Angels* and that you and your family enjoy a very joyous Christmas.

Mia Jha

A VIEW FOR FIRST-TIME READERS

This introduction contains minimal plot-spoilers.

Elizabeth Goudge's short novel, *Sister of the Angels* (1939), is the second in a series sometimes known as 'The Torminster Trilogy', named after the fictional cathedral city of Torminster, in Devon, England. Like the other novels in the trilogy, it is based, to some extent, on aspects of Elizabeth Goudge's childhood up to the age of eleven, when her father, Henry Goudge, an ordained Church of England priest, was a post-secondary lecturer and vice-dean in the theological college of Wells Cathedral. (For US readers: the Church of England is equivalent to the Episcopal Church.)

Sister of the Angels is Elizabeth Goudge's fifth novel and arguably her first children's novel—the first of eight novels written for children—but it is also deeply satisfying for adult readers. It is a short novel, with 145 numbered pages in my American first edition, including ten full-page illustrations that are blank on the reverse of the pages. Hence the book contains about 125 pages of text, presented as nine numbered chapters. Nonetheless, although it might be referred to as a novelette, I do not think it should be classified as a (long) short story.

Most people interested in *Sister of the Angels* or about to read this GGBP edition will already be familiar with other novels by Goudge. Some may be enthusiasts who have been rereading her books throughout much of their lives. Many will already be familiar with *A City of Bells* (1936), the first in 'The Torminster Trilogy', and they will be eager to read the sequel, learning more about the remarkable characters in that opening novel. Readers already familiar with Goudge's work who are about to read *Sister of the Angels* for the first time may need little introduction to this short novel. After they have read it, some retrospective notes may enhance their enjoyment of the book.

But what could a novel that is more than eighty years old offer modern readers who know nothing, or little, about Elizabeth Goudge and her works? What can first-time readers of *Sister of the Angels* look forward to? What would interest possible first-time readers?

They might be interested in sisters? Or in angels? Or intrigued by the possibility that angels might have sisters? Like many of Goudge's titles, this one does not tell, or even indicate, a story. But once the novel has been read the significance of the title is obvious.

What will first-time readers find in *Sister of the Angels*, especially first-time Goudge readers? Like many of Goudge's novels, it seems simple, but it is surprisingly rich in detail, and full of her special kind of suspense. You will find yourself several times turning back to an earlier page when some half-remembered trivial detail suddenly turns out not to be trivial at all. Goudge writes subtle stories with multiple narrative strands that connect unexpectedly. You may also feel confident that you can guess the—predictably happy—ending. But you will be in suspense, wondering how it will occur.

There is humour. Not laugh-out-loud side-splitting humour: gentle, wry moments that move you emotionally while also amusing you. For example, early in the story, after getting up in the wintery morning, with the first snow falling outside, and no heating in her ice-cold bedroom, and the agonising requirement of washing herself with a can of warm water, Henrietta notices that her adoptive brother, Hugh Anthony, seems to have neglected washing himself. She asks his two white mice, Hengist and Horsa, 'How much did he wash?' But they 'said nothing but looked very sad' (p65). This is a realistic novel, and animals cannot talk, of course. But in Goudge's world, animals communicate, or seem to, without words. And, indeed, in *Smoky House* (1941), some of the animals actually talk to one another! But that is a story that also includes fairies, so the fantasy of talking animals seems natural. *The Little White Horse* (1946) has a cat that can write messages with its tail.

Later, Henrietta rushes to the railway station to meet her father, 'skidding into fat old gentlemen and sending them staggering into the heaps of snow beside the gutter'. Then she is delayed for five minutes after a collision with the Archdeacon, 'for you must stop to pick up an Archdeacon when you knock him over' (p94). The slapstick is amusing, and the life-rule about how to treat Archdeacons is a small joke, but is typical of Goudge's deft touch. Even the names of some of the minor characters are amusing, such as the head verger (a lay worker in the cathedral), Peppercorn, and Mr Gotobed, 'the portly worthy' who drove 'the old pumpkin-shaped horse bus' (p96). Both Peppercorn and Gotobed are actual surnames, however quaintly amusing they may seem to modern readers—and Goudge.

Henrietta's octogenarian adoptive 'mother', Jane Fordyce, wife of Canon Fordyce of Torminster Cathedral, known by Henrietta as 'Grandmother', has the heart of a saint, but tends to be strict and stern. At a potentially difficult moment in the story when Grandmother might have made strenuous objections to a suggested course of action, she makes no objection at all, to everybody else's considerable surprise. Why? She had 'just turned the heel of her sock' and was 'in an exceptionally good mood' (p145). Anyone familiar with knitting, especially the knitting of socks, and the challenge of creating the change of direction, the heel, between the ankle section and the foot section, will smile at this moment. Goudge's sense of humour can be very subtle.

There are narrative layers. Leaving aside the fact that *Sister of the*

Angels is a sequel, as a self-contained story it includes events from millennia earlier, centuries earlier, decades earlier. (It even mentions Adam in the Garden of Eden!) Moreover, its setting, around 1910, sometimes demands that modern readers understand that life more than one hundred years ago was very different, in many ways, from modern life, and make adjustments for things that an English author writing in 1939 would naturally take for granted. (Pre-television. Pre-radio. Pre-Internet. A primitive early automobile in *Henrietta's House* is a startling outrage!) It may help to read Goudge as though she is Jane Austen, or Charles Dickens writing in a light mood, or Louisa May Alcott, or Frances Hodgson Burnett. You are reading about your ancestors four or five generations ago. This should not be off-putting. They are delightful ancestors.

As with all of Goudge's writing, *Sister of the Angels* quotes, refers to, and alludes to other writers and books, art and artists, music, and diverse culture. Traditional Christmas carols, for example, Hengist and Horsa, the Book of Common Prayer (fleetingly), Sherlock Holmes, and Early Renaissance art in Italy. The English king Henry VIII is mentioned, as 'bluff King Hal' who 'destroyed the monastery and the monks fled' (p84). Henry VIII's invention of the Church of England (part of the Reformation) may have been necessary for his dynastic succession, and his divorces, as a way to avoid the political control of the Pope. The sale of the Catholic monasteries added to his coffers. It was also a crucial, nation-building step towards separating the state from the Roman Catholic church. But it came at a terrible cost to vibrant, prosperous religious communities, with great destruction to abbeys, monasteries, and convents. Despite this, Henry preserved many parish churches and cathedrals to be used by the newly created Church of England clergy and congregations. This, and much more, is implicit in the narrative's few words: 'bluff King Hal [who] destroyed the monastery'. The word 'bluff' may be traditional, for Henry VIII, but in this context is ironic.

In short, Goudge, here and in her other books, always writes from a deeply informed background, which she assumes will be broadly familiar to her readers. School curriculums have changed since her time, and modern readers need to be well informed to grasp the worlds of Goudge and her characters, just as do modern readers dealing with Jane Austen, Emily Brontë, or, more recently, Graham Greene.

As with many other Goudge novels, *Sister of the Angels* includes animals, family pets. As well as the historically named pair of white mice, Hengist and Horsa (do you know the history?), there is Charles the tortoise; a carved stone dog, that Henrietta names 'Eric', on a memorial statue in the cathedral; and Cornelia, the mother cat in the sweet shop, with an endless stream of kittens, including one black kitten who is 'administered' to Henrietta, like a dose of medicine, by her father, when she is distressed in her meeting with a mysterious artist who is to paint her portrait (p125).

There is also food. Goudge's books highlight food and meals. Sausages (for breakfast!), eggs and bacon, steak and kidney (probably in a pie), baked apple (typically with some cloves and brown sugar where the core has been removed), water biscuits (these are water crackers in America) and Cheddar cheese, hot lemon drink, honey, satin prauleens (an eccentric or obsolete name for 'delicious squares of coloured sugar, hard outside and soft inside', p124), marmalade, sausage rolls (which may be unfamiliar to American readers, but consist of herbed or spiced finely ground meat wrapped in a coat of flaky pastry and baked), and jelly (which American readers would know as Jell-O).

Another key element in *Sister of the Angels*, and all of Goudge's books, is Christianity. This is natural, and inevitable, in a book where Grandfather, who adopted Henrietta, is a Canon of Torminster Cathedral. He is a man who insists on Grace being said, and properly observed by a rather naughty hungry grandson, before eating, and who agonises over a young man's desperate acts when he tries to support his brothers and sisters—this central thread has a hint of Victor Hugo's 'Jean Valjean', from *Les Miserables*. One of the main themes of *Sister of the Angels* is redemption of a person who has committed a crime—sinned.

Henrietta's concern for the carved Virgin and Child over the west door of the cathedral, covered in snow, causes her to say, 'I wish we could bring him inside ... I'm afraid he'll catch cold out there' (p74). Then, inside the cathedral, she sees another statue of the Virgin and Child high up at the end of the nave, caught in 'a shaft of sunlight, shining through a clerestory window, lit ... up with such a golden glory that it seemed like a lamp shining in the heart of the shadowy Cathedral' (p75).

Later, when Henrietta returns to the cathedral for the Christmas Eve carol service in the crypt, she feels the warmth of the stoves heating the building. 'If only she could pick up armfuls of the warmth and comfort, carry it to the west door and fling it outside across the snow to the figures who toiled out there alone in the cold' (p140). At this point she remembers a vision she had experienced 'weeks ago', of a man 'toiling across a snowy moor and until this moment had quite forgotten' (p141). Readers have probably 'quite forgotten' Henrietta's vision, and will search back for an incident, and a memory, that at first had probably seemed trivial detail. Henrietta had been listening to Hugh Anthony's spontaneously invented far-fetched story of a convict released from his sentence in the bleak prison at Dartmoor: her imagination and high sensitivity had inspired her (pp66, 67).

In the warm cathedral, remembering her earlier vision:

> She was suddenly glad that she had not been able to bring the snowy statue of the Child inside with her. She was glad he was outside with those who were cold and desolate as well

as inside with the warm and comforted. (p141)

But despite such moments of emotion, this is not a pious or preachy book. Goudge includes Christianity and Christian morals in a simple, traditional, non-denominational way, drawing on it for support in moments of personal existential crisis. Life sometimes treats a person badly. But the bad days pass by (p97). The theme of consolation—that, however bad something is right now, it will come to an end—recurs in some of Goudge's later adult novels, such as *The Rosemary Tree* (1956) and *The Scent of Water* (1963), and in her children's novel *The Little White Horse* (1946). This consolation is also the source of the happy endings in other Goudge books, even the bleakest, such as her World War II novel, *The Castle on the Hill* (1942).

First-time readers of *Sister of the Angels* can look forward to a moving story with charming and often amusing characters, and important and engaging matters. And there is a sequel, and a prequel!

John Gough

A VIEW FOR EXPERIENCED
GOUDGE READERS

WARNING: this introduction contains MAJOR PLOT-SPOILERS.

(In references to Sister of the Angels, page numbers are for this new GGBP edition. Page numbers for Henrietta's House refer to the GGBP edition of 2013, reprinted 2020 and 2021.)

Looking at *Sister of the Angels* (1939) within the body of Goudge's work, or rereading this novel, there are three main narrative threads in it: the historical story of Saint Nicolas de Malden and the Medieval crypt and wall paintings, Nicolas Broadbent's restoration of the original paintings, and Henrietta's present story. Behind these human stories is the Christian story of Christ's birth, and, implicitly, his life, death and resurrection, and, explicitly, the promise of Judgement Day. The novel even briefly looks back, wryly, to Adam shortly after he is created.

Clearly, *Sister of the Angels* is a sequel to *A City of Bells* (1935). Importantly, it centres on the long-ago story of Nicolas de Malden, the monk who was an artist, 'and the greatest missal painter of his time, famous all over Europe for the glory of his art' (p83), who became a leper, and isolated himself in the crypt beneath Torminster Cathedral, and created three astounding painted walls—'heaven and earth and hell' (p84)—Judgment Day, the Second Coming, and Christ in Majesty—but dying before he could paint the fourth wall. (A missal is a Mass book, containing the instructions and texts for celebrating the sacrament of the Mass—that is, Holy Communion, or the Eucharist, the church service modelled on the Last Supper that Jesus celebrated with his chosen disciples before he was betrayed to the Romans.)

In fact, Nicolas de Malden, and the whole story of *Sister of the Angels*, is the development of an uncanny passage in *A City of Bells*, where Henrietta returns to Torminster after spending time in London with her adoptive uncle, Jocelyn Fordyce, and his actress wife, and experiencing the triumph of Gabriel Ferranti's romantic verse drama, *The Minstrel.* Henrietta joyfully reunites with Hugh Anthony, her adoptive younger brother, and his new guinea-pig, Solomon, and the rest of her family and domestic household. There is high tea—a special late afternoon or early evening meal with many different foods. (Surprisingly, here, Goudge, who usually revels in listing and describing what people eat, says nothing more than 'high tea'.) And Henrietta unpacks after her trip to London:

... and then at last she was alone in her scented bedroom with the carved angels [as later described in the first scene of *Sister of the Angels*], standing on the bare floor in her nightgown and listening to a spring shower pattering down on the garden path outside her window ... And mingling with the shower was the sound of footsteps coming clack-clack up the stairs and along the passage.

Henrietta smiled, for she knew who it was. It was the lovely lady with the powdered hair and the great billowing rosy skirt and the green petticoat, who had rings on her fingers and a black patch on her chin and pattered up and down the stairs in the evening when the house was quiet. Henrietta opened her door very softly and peeped out, but she could not see anything or hear anything now but a mouse. It was funny how she could never see that lady with her bodily eyes, but only the eyes of her mind, and that so clearly that she could describe her appearance down to the smallest detail. (*A City of Bells,* Chapter XII, Part I, pp253–254; ellipsis in the original)

We are teetering on the verge of the supernatural here, because it is clear that what Henrietta has heard, and vividly seen in her mind's eye, is the ghost of an eighteenth-century lady with powdered hair and a very fashionable pasted-on beauty spot. The strength of Henrietta's visual imagination is a theme through *A City of Bells.* But the suggestion is that there are two aspects of a person, one seeing and hearing with bodily eyes and ears, and another seeing and hearing otherwise hidden, unseen truths, ideals, spirits. This is a Goudgean theme that first appeared in her first novel, *Island Magic* (1934), with Michelle, a sensitive, clever girl similar to Henrietta, and it recurs in many later novels. But the word 'ghost' is not mentioned. Goudge believed in ghosts and extra-sensory perception (ESP) and discussed this, and her mother's spiritual sensitivity, in *The Joy of the Snow* (Chapter VII, 'E.S.P.').

But there is more!

She tiptoed down the passage and opened the door of the spare-room. No one was sleeping there now and the furniture was shrouded with dust-sheets and the curtains drawn. The light was so dim that it must have been difficult for the man who sat there painting to see what he was doing. She could hardly see him herself though she knew so well what he looked like ... He had a kind, lined face and a circular bald patch on the top of his head, and he wore a long brown robe that reached to his toes and a rope around his middle ... He was painting a book, ornamenting its pages with purple pansies and ivory roses and queer little animals with long legs and scarlet tongues ... It was strange that she knew all about

19

that book though she only saw it in the dark. (*A City of Bells*, Chapter XII, Part I, p254; ellipsis in the original)

Again, the word 'ghost' is not mentioned, but is clearly implied. In the dark spare-room Henrietta has seen (somehow, mysteriously, because of the darkness), not for the first time, a tonsured monk painting—illuminating in the margins—a missal! The monk is not named. Readers of *Sister of the Angels* know he is Nicolas de Malden, and a ghost.

When [Henrietta] had been younger, quite a little girl, she had sometimes seen a ghost in that room [the spare room now occupied by her father while he visits for Christmas], a grey monk who sat painting gay flowers and birds and beasts in the margin of a big book. She had never been frightened of him, for always he had been absorbed and happy, and seemingly quite unaware of her presence ... Grandfather had said that he wasn't a real man at all, but just a sort of photograph of the past, a photograph of a real man who had once sat in his [monastery] cell, built where their spare room was now, painting as she saw him paint. (*Sister of the Angels*, p116: Grandfather's explanation is a variant of the explanations Goudge provides in *The Joy of the Snow*, Chapter VI 'E.S.P.')

Missals feature later in *Sister of the Angels*, when we learn that Hugh Anthony and Grandfather have secretly made painted decorations for Ferranti's big Christmas tree:

with little figures of angels and beasts, birds and flowers, cut out of pictures and mounted upon cardboard, and as like as Grandfather and Hugh Anthony could get them to the old missals that Nicolas de Malden used to paint. (pp138-139;

also hinted at earlier, p121)

In passing, it may be noted that the narrator uses an old-fashioned and politically incorrect (by modern standards) idiom. 'The Christmas tree was superb and Grandfather and Hugh Anthony must have worked like blacks to decorate it' (p138). Modern readers will see this and, surely, cry 'racism'! But this is in a book written in 1939, by a woman born in Queen Victoria's reign. Such an expression was as common as saying 'they must have worked like Trojans', which is always intended as a compliment, and is in no way an ethnic slur on Trojans. Moreover, if we consider Goudge's context, this is not in the least demeaning or racist. Instead, this is very positive, and affirming. It is high praise for Grandfather and Hugh Anthony: their hard work is outstanding. By implication, also, the hard-working 'blacks' in the expression are clearly also doing very well. They are praiseworthy exemplars of hard work. Goudge needs to be read carefully, closely, and with awareness of her era and her character. She was not in the slightest way a racist.

In her detailed biography, *Beyond the Snow: The Life and Faith of Elizabeth Goudge* (2015), Christine Rawlins also notes several Goudgean connections and themes in *Sister of the Angels*. For example, Gabriel Ferranti explains to Henrietta why he has commissioned an artist to paint her portrait:

I was once in a mess myself, and Grandfather and other people helped me out. I can't repay my debt to the people to whom I really owe it, one seldom can in this world, but I can in a sense repay it to somebody else. (p115)

Rawlins (p209) points out how this theme, most recently popularised in *Pay It Forward*, the 1999 novel by Catherine Ryan Hyde and the 2000 movie of the same title, appeared earlier in

21

Goudge's historical novel *Towers in the Mist* (1938), and later in *Gentian Hill* (1949). A version of this repayment transferred forwards also occurs in Goudge's second-last adult novel, *The Scent of Water* (1963), as Cousin Mary plans ahead to help Mary Lindsay, and Mary Lindsay herself then helps Edith Talbot, the adopted daughter of her neighbours.

Rawlins also notes that *Sister of the Angels* was published, without Hodges' illustrations, in the 1939 December edition of *Woman's Journal*, under the title 'The Constant Heart'.

Another Goudgean theme is the image and experience of depths that sustain a troubled person. As the artist (Nicolas Broadbent, or John Henry Barnes, although at this point Henrietta does not know him by name) is painting Henrietta's portrait he reflects:

> He had thought that he would never paint again [after the trauma of imprisonment], but this peace [working in a makeshift studio above the sweet-shop in the Torminster Market Place] was like a deep well; down at the bottom of it the waters of inspiration sprang up unchanged. (p131)

Rachell, in *Island Magic* (1934), has a similar experience as she rests and, in a way, prays or meditates on her bed after lunch. Henrietta also knows this experience as an artist, when she feels something like a 'click' in her head when she concentrates her attention upon some absorbing task, and she has seen it in others (pp127, 131). We might say, in the modern terms of positive psychology, that she is in a 'flow state' or 'in the zone'. In *The Rosemary Tree* (1956), Daphne Wentworth finds this peace, waiting in her husband's parish church, imagining the deep rock beneath the church supporting her. A well is the secret key to Maria Merryweather undoing the curse on Moonacre in *The Little White Horse* (1946), which also has a spring, as do *Island Magic* (1934) and *The Castle on the Hill* (1942). Water rising—springing!—out of the ground is a potent image for Goudge.

Interestingly, as sequels to *A City of Bells*, some problems in narrative chronology appear when we carefully compare *Sister of the Angels*, published in 1939, and *Henrietta's House*, published in 1942 (reissued in 2013 by GGBP), which is approximately twice as long as *Sister of the Angels*. (*Henrietta's House* is known as *The Blue Hills* in America.) For example, in the earlier published sequel, *Sister of the Angels*, Henrietta is eleven years old (p62), her adoptive brother Hugh Anthony is ten years old (p71), and Grandfather is eighty (p70). By contrast, in *Henrietta's House*, published later, Henrietta is ten years old (p53, GGBP edition), Hugh Anthony is initially about nine and then has a birthday that features prominently in the story, and Grandfather is seventy-nine (p78, GGBP edition). However, Grandmother is resolutely eighty-two in both books (*Henrietta's House*, p55, GGBP edition; *Sister of the Angels*, p70). In *A City of Bells* (1935), Henrietta is ten, and Hugh Anthony is eight. But *Sister of the Angels* tells us Henrietta is 'his elder by a year' (p65).

In *Sister of the Angels*, Hugh Anthony is attending a day school in Torminster because Grandfather does not have enough money to pay for a boarding school that would, perhaps, assist with curbing his youthful exuberance. Grandfather is charitable almost to excess, and has given away a legacy (money inherited from someone or somewhere) 'to persons unknown' (p72). Then, later, in *Henrietta's House*, we learn that Hugh Anthony is returning for the summer school holidays, after his first term at the boarding school he has been sent to recently (p54, GGBP edition). (Many online commentators claim the school is Eton, but I have not seen this in my English editions of *Henrietta's House*, where it is described as a 'preparatory school'—which Eton certainly is not. Perhaps they are confused because he wears an Eton collar.) Hugh Anthony's schooling is clearly sequential across the novels. In *A City of Bells* he and Henrietta are being taught by Miss Lavender. She is a woman who has never taught anything but Sunday-school, but generous Grandfather knows that this income (he secretly overpays her) will help her (*A City of Bells*, Chapter III, Part I, p59).

In *Henrietta's House*, Henrietta is described as artistic, but with the author's tongue firmly in cheek. Exploring the mysterious house that gives the novel its title, Henrietta sighs with ecstasy as she opens a red lacquer desk and sees a large paintbox, a box full of camel-hair brushes, a box full of pencils and rubbers and a stack of drawing paper.

> She was an artist of no mean order, one of those accomplished persons who can draw a pig to look like a pig and not like a balloon with a piece of twisted string poking out behind. (p205, GGBP edition)

By contrast, in *Sister of the Angels*, this 'artist of no mean order', who can draw a recognisable pig that is distinguishable from a balloon and a piece of twisted string, is able to make a sketch of a Nativity scene that, amazingly, exactly matches the idea of a professional artist for a Nativity to be painted on the east wall of the chapel beneath the cathedral. Moreover, when the artist actually paints the mural, Henrietta is allowed to help paint some of the drapery, and the detail of the little dog, modelled on a memorial carving in the cathedral, a stone dog Henrietta calls Eric (pp91, 132-133).

Henrietta also spends time making a book, to be a Christmas present for Grandfather, painting 'all the angels she had ever heard about', including the four warrior archangels, Michael, Gabriel, Raphael and Asrael, and seraphs with six wings, and guardian angels who are 'less well dressed than the others, a little overworked and harassed because their human charges gave them such a lot of trouble', and 'jolly fat little bodiless cherubs like the carvings in her room' (p135). Clearly, in the book written earlier Henrietta is artistically capable of far more than a pig that does not look like a balloon! Angels and seraphs also feature in other novels such as *Island Magic* and *The Rosemary Tree*.

Remarkably, in *A City of Bells* (1936), with no thought of any sequel, Goudge several times described Henrietta as having a rich dream life, an intense sensitivity to colours, scents, and sounds, and a vivid imagination. 'One day she too would make something and it should be beautiful' (*A City of Bells*, Chapter XII, Part III, p265). 'Later on in her life, when she grew up, ... she learnt how to paint her dreams with a brush on canvas so that other people saw them too.' (*A City of Bells*, Chapter II, Part II, p42). And:

> ... years later she painted a picture full of queer spirals that created a great sensation in artistic circles but was never completely understood. (*A City of Bells*, Chapter II, Part III, p46)

The accounts of Henrietta's interest and ability in art are inconsistent across the three Torminster novels. But in the character of Henrietta, Goudge was almost certainly creating a successful version of herself as artist. Goudge had trained in art and crafts and worked as an art teacher, but was largely a failure in her art studies, and could only manage to paint still-life pictures of flowers with any success (*The Joy of the Snow*, Chapter VIII 'Non-Education', Part 6, pp160–163).

In *Sister of the Angels*, we read:

> Henrietta ... was attached to her sleep, both because it made her feel refreshed and strong, and because in it she visited wonderful places, saw lovely sights and heard wonderful sounds. (p120; Rawlins mentions this, p264)

Dreams are an important Goudgean theme in other novels, including *The Little White Horse* and *The Scent of Water*. Moreover, dreams were important for Goudge. She discusses them twice in *The Joy of the Snow* (Chapter VII 'E.S.P.', Part 3, pp131–132, and Part 5, pp140–144.) Goudge also discusses them in an essay, 'Dreams', included in the collection *At the Sign of the Dolphin* (1947: also known as *The Elizabeth Goudge Reader*), as mentioned by Christine Rawlins (pp227–228), linking this with a dream of a flight of birds at dawn, early in *The Rosemary Tree*.

In her essay 'Dreams', Goudge describes a special recurring dream she had:

> I am a little girl again, jogging along in the old-fashioned cab that in my childhood [at Wells] we used to hire to take us to parties. Again I am gloriously happy, for that sense of expectancy [also in another recurring dream of walking along a path towards something wonderful] is with me again, and looking out of the window of the cab I see a lovely landscape of green hills bathed in that special light … The ground rises gently to thick beech woods, and with its back to the woods and facing the stream there is a long low white house. ('Dreams': quoted from Rawlins, p241)

From this dream, and Goudge's childhood memories of Wells, came *Henrietta's House*, with an old-fashioned carriage ride towards a birthday picnic, and so much more!

Similarly, the image of the little white horse first appeared to Goudge in a dream. She explains this in 'West Country Magic' (*Horn Book*, March 1947, following winning the Carnegie Medal for *The Little White Horse*), saying that the landscape of Devon had been a big inspiration for the book:

> Not far away [from where Goudge and her mother lived,
> in Devon, during World War II] there is a beautiful cove
> where the white horses from the sea come galloping in …
> One night I dreamed that one of them galloped inland and
> did not go back. (Quoted in Rawlins, p264)

Incidentally, Henrietta believes that she is tall for her age, eleven (p125). But on the first page of *Henrietta's House* we are told 'she was small for ten years old'.

Interestingly, in *Sister of the Angels*, the slapstick comedy of Gabriel Ferranti, Henrietta's eccentric Italian poet father, arriving at Torminster railway station clutching a Christmas tree* with a large bag of oranges in the other hand, evokes memories of earlier events:

> Ferranti's eccentric arrivals were always popular at the station
> for there was no knowing what he might bring with him as a
> present for the children; Hengist and Horsa the white mice,
> a puppy in a basket, a bowl of goldfish, a talking parrot; all
> these had arrived at various times and had given great pleasure
> at the station, though not to Grandmother later on. (p95)

But, amazingly, in *Henrietta's House*, published three years later, the mysterious arrival at the railway station of a hamper that contains an unlabelled puppy is the start of the adventure. Henrietta resolves to

---

*which C Walter Hodges's illustration on page 138 shows to be unclutchably large; also, surprisingly, Hodges puts an angel on top of the tree, whereas the text says a 'great silver star [was] on the top'; just as surprisingly, Hodges shows Grandfather clean-shaven on page 68, but the text on pages 70 and 72 says he has a white beard; nor is Grandmother shown wearing a lace cap—oops!

steal the puppy, and for much of the rest of the novel she agonises guiltily over the sinfulness of her dog-snatching. ('Thou shalt not steal' is one of the Ten Commandments! Henrietta is unusually sensitive, and pious, and takes sin very seriously.)

In the second-last chapter, Gabriel Ferranti tells Henrietta that Keeper, as Hugh Anthony has named the puppy (honouring his namesake, the original, legendary Saint Hugh of Torminster, who was a swineherd and had a dog to mind his pigs: *Henrietta's House*, p61, GGBP edition; also, Saint Anthony the Great had a pig, and is the patron saint of pig keepers), had actually been sent by Ferranti to Henrietta—but the puppy chewed the label.

"Then when I stole Keeper for Hugh Anthony [who wanted to have a dog, against Grandmother's wishes] on the platform at Torminster Station I was *stealing my own dog*!" she cried joyfully. "Oh, Grandfather, does that mean that I am not a thief after all?"

Grandfather, who was sitting on the other side of the Old Gentleman [who gave his house to Henrietta], laid down his knife and fork and looked a little troubled. "I am not sure, Henrietta," he said. "Your question has raised something of a theological problem. I am rather inclined to think that if you *thought* you were stealing when you took Keeper then you *were* stealing, even though unknown to yourself Keeper was your own." [The Old Man, who has been persuaded to stop sticking pins into wax dolls to cause harm, and has found his misplaced heart—his story is another thread in the complicated plot of the novel—objects, defending Henrietta. Grandfather insists the Old Man is, speaking theologically, wrong. But he relents, a little.]

"And certainly sins committed for love are half-way to becoming virtues, and so, Henrietta, we'll say no more about

it." (*Henrietta's House,* pp256–257, GGBP edition: italics in
the original)

Henrietta's House is a remarkable book—written for children!—
that insists on theological precision at a moment of moral crisis. But
is Keeper the dog that, reportedly, Ferranti had sent—earlier?—to
the children in *Sister of the Angels*?

These minor anomalies may have been ironed out in the later
revising of *Henrietta's House* when a new edition was made with fresh
illustrations by Antony Maitland.

Perhaps crucially, in 1939, as Goudge wrote *Sister of the Angels*, she
was struggling with grief following her father's sudden death, with
the distress of having to move from Oxford, with the uncertainties
and dangers of the mounting threat of war, and then the declaration
of war on 3 September 1939, and the need to find a suitable house
for herself and her chronically invalid, and ill, mother. Goudge
was also working very hard to earn a living from her writing, to
support herself and her mother. Some allowance must be made if,
at times, Goudge has not scrupulously married *A City of Bells* with
its urgently written sequel, *Sister of the Angels*, while also completing
the first 'Dameroshay' novel, *The Bird in the Tree* (1940). She would
have been exhausted, but could not afford to relax.

Incidentally, it may be noted that twice in *Sister of the Angels*
Goudge used words that have now changed their meaning.
Describing eccentric Gabriel Ferranti, who Henrietta several times
thinks of as a kind of Pied Piper, Goudge mentions his 'gay mad
clothes' (p97). Here the word 'gay' does not have the modern
meaning, 'homosexual', but has the older meanings of 'bright',
'cheerful', 'happy'. Earlier, encountering a strange man in Torminster
Cathedral, glimpsed fleetingly when Henrietta enters the building
(she is actually meeting Nicolas Broadbent for the first time, but
does not learn his name until much later), she, or the narrator,

describes him having 'a queer voice, husky and very slow' (p79). The meaning of 'queer' has also changed since Goudge wrote. Here it does not have the modern meaning of 'homosexual'. Instead it means 'unusual', 'eccentric', 'strange'.

Note that a Cathedral Close is, traditionally, the small community of houses beside a cathedral, occupied by the religious members and lay workers of the cathedral, and their families. These were, and often still are, contained within—enclosed by—a wall.

The title, *Sister of the Angels*, deserves some discussion. It reveals nothing to a prospective reader. As a contrasting example, the alternative title used in the Swiss-German translation, *Henriettas Weihnachten* (1957, published in Zurich), immediately makes a connection, for readers familiar with *A City of Bells*, by naming the central character, Henrietta. Also, for German readers, it highlights the importance of the time of the year in the story, Christmas, because 'Weihnachten' is the German word for 'Christmas'. Moreover, this German-language title parallels the title of the third novel in the trilogy, *Henrietta's House*.

Unfortunately, the German alternative title loses Henrietta's witty use of 'Fra Angelico' as her nickname for the artist introduced to her by her father. The artist has been commissioned to paint her portrait, to be a Christmas present for her adoptive Grandfather. He will also paint the mural on the east wall of the underground chapel in Torminster Cathedral, completing the medieval wall paintings of Nicolas de Malden. Henrietta asks the artist what she should call him, and he suggests his actual name, 'John'. But Henrietta does not think that would be a sufficiently respectful way for an eleven-year-old to address an adult who seems much older than her. She suggests calling him 'Fra Angelico', after the great Dominican friar who was a major artist in the Early Renaissance. Henrietta explains, 'They called him the Brother of the Angels because he painted angels so beautifully' (p127).

This is a touching tribute from Henrietta, and Goudge, as author.

But the Italian nickname actually means 'Angelic Friar'. (The word 'Fra' derives from the Latin word 'frater', meaning 'brother'.) The nickname began to be used posthumously by fellow monks and artists as a tribute to the friar's deep spirituality. Nevertheless, it is a touching mistake for Henrietta to make. In turn, the artist recognises Henrietta's precocious talent—he has seen her pencil sketch for the east wall, and admires it, knowing it is virtually identical to his own ideas—and, in turn, he addresses her as 'Suora Angelico' (p133)— hence the title of the novel.

In conclusion, it is important to consider the emotional and narrative heart of *Sister of the Angels*. Henrietta is, arguably, the main character—the character of the title—with most of the story seen through her eyes and experience. Despite this, the focus of the story is compassion for, and redemption of, a convicted criminal, with the consequence—the climax—that Nicolas Broadbent (in fact this is not his real name) rediscovers his creativity and confidence, and completes the restoration of Nicolas de Malden's murals with the fourth wall painting. Compassion for criminals, and their redemption and return to society, is a Goudgean theme that recurs, later, in *The Rosemary Tree* (1956) and *The Scent of Water* (1963). It is part of Goudge's social awareness and Christian charity, shared with her father and his engagement with working-class people, poverty and social justice.

Sister of the Angels is a striking, heart-warming book, to be savoured.

John Gough

TOWER HOUSE, WELLS

Elizabeth Goudge lived in two clerical houses in Wells, in St Andrew Street. The first was Tower House, which was her parents' first married home, and it was there she was born, on 24 April 1900, and spent her first two or three years. The second, the Principal's House, now called The Rib, was across the road; the Goudges moved there when the Reverend Henry Goudge was appointed principal of the theological college. Some decades ago the Diocese of Bath and Wells sold the medieval clergy homes in St Andrew Street, and they are now in private ownership.

As she herself told us in *The Joy of the Snow* (p7), 'When I wrote *A City of Bells* I placed my family in Tower House but fetched the cherub population from across the road to be with them'. The Tower House of her imagination is described by Canon Fordyce in *A City of Bells* when Jocelyn asks him how old the house is. His grandfather replies, 'It belongs to all time. The Hall and kitchen and larder are Norman, the tower is fifteenth century and this room has an eighteenth century powdering closet.' (p25). It should be noted that what Elizabeth Goudge thought was an 'an eighteenth century powdering closet' was a medieval lavatory! In *The Joy of the Snow* Elizabeth remembers that: 'To enter Tower House, down steps into a cool dark hall was like going into a cave and it had, as its name implies, a stone tower with little rooms like monastic cells leading from the spiral stone staircase' (p6). There is no mention in the Cathedral's historical records of a Norman house, and the first recorded occupant was M Henry de Schavington, Archdeacon of Taunton, in 1323 (see Sherwin Bailey's *Canonical House of Wells*, 1982). However, it is possible that there may have been a house on the site in Norman times, for there has been a cathedral in Wells since 909, and the 14th-century house, as was often the case, could have been built over part of an earlier building's foundations, which would explain why Elizabeth remembers stepping down into the hall. There was no monastic foundation in Wells. That was in nearby Glastonbury, just over six miles away, which was one of the greatest and most powerful monastic sites in medieval England.

Elizabeth admitted in *The Joy of the Snow* (p7) that like so many authors she changes the real places that inspired her: 'This seems the place to apologise for a maddening habit of which I think most novelists are guilty. We give a story the setting of a place or countryside that we love but we are not accurate. Our memories go down into the subconsciousness, get overlaid with one thing and another and are fished up again anyhow and pieced together with the glue of sheer inventiveness.'

Nearly 500 years have passed since the Protestant Reformation, and the two houses will have been altered many times by the Anglican clergy who lived there—for example, in the 18th century, in Tower House, Tudor panelling was added to the walls of the Angel Room. Tower House, under the present owner, who has lived there for 50 years, has had almost no alteration. The main difference that Elizabeth would note is that the house is a little warmer. Tower House and the Rib are now Grade 2* listed, which means that the owners are restricted these days in what they can do.

We are extremely grateful to Mrs Pamela Egan, the current owner of Tower House, for graciously sending us two photographs, taken by her daughter Vicky Egan, of medieval features that still exist and which Elizabeth and her parents would have known. These are a stone angel carving (see page 32) and a piscina (see facing page and below), which is a stone basin near the altar in Catholic and pre-Reformation churches for draining water used in the Mass. This tells us that the room was originally a chapel where the occupant of the time, who would have been the Precentor, one of the Cathedral's senior clergy, would have celebrated a private Mass.

Ann Mackie-Hunter

THE GRAVE, WITH MEMORIAL CROSS, AS IT WAS IN 2001

ELIZABETH GOUDGE'S GRAVE

In 2020, when GGBP first published *The World of Elizabeth Goudge* by Sylvia Gower, we discovered that the Goudge family grave no longer had its cross. Opposite you will see the grave as it was in 2001, and on pages 38 and 39 you will see the grave as it is now.

We decided that we should organise a Just Giving page in order to raise funds to have a new cross put on the grave. We still have not raised enough money, and so if you are interested in contributing to that, please go to the Elizabeth Goudge page on our website, www. ggbp.co.uk/authors-and-series/elizabeth-goudge/, and you will find the details. If you would like to donate but are unable to do this yourself, please do not send any money to GGBP but ask a friend or relative to donate on the Just Giving page for you.

Clarissa Cridland

THE GOUDGE GRAVE AS IT IS (2020)
BOTTOM RIGHT SHOWS ELIZABETH GOUDGE'S MEMORIAL STONE.

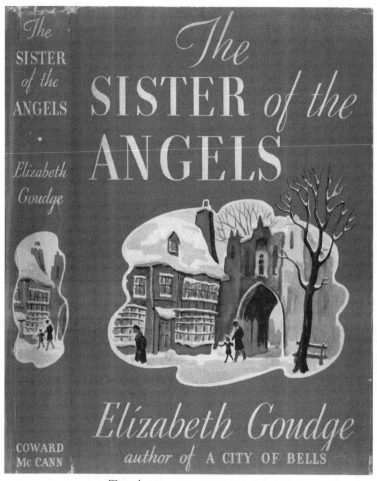

THE AMERICAN FIRST EDITION,
PUBLISHED BY COWARD MCCANN IN 1939

PUBLISHING HISTORY

Sister of the Angels was first published by Gerald Duckworth & Co Ltd in hardback in 1939. It had black-and-white line illustrations by C Walter Hodges, all of which we have reproduced in this GGBP edition. Hodges also provided the illustration for the front of the dustwrapper, which we have used for our own front cover; the spine is reproduced on the back cover. This edition was reprinted in 1943, 1947, 1948 and 1954. As far as I am aware, the boards underneath the dustwrapper were plain, although they seem to have varied in colour.

There was a Guild Book (bookclub I think) edition (see page 43), but I have no date for this.

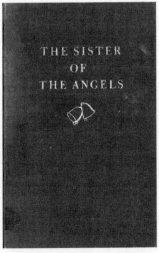

A later reprint came from Duckworth, in 1976 (see page 44), 'the Christchurch edition', which follows the same format as other Elizabeth Goudge titles.

In the USA, Coward McCann published *Sister of the Angels* in 1939. The dustwrapper, seen opposite, has a lovely blue background colour. And the front of the boards, which were otherwise plain blue, had two bells. This edition, like all American editions, was entitled <u>*The*</u> *Sister of the Angels*. NB, I did find the front of the wrapper of this edition on the Internet as being published by Duckworth in 1947, which is quite incorrect. It is with thanks to John Gough that I have been able to identify it. I have also just discovered an edition with different boards (see page 52). It may be that this was for a later edition, or it may be that sheets (pages) of the first printing were held and used later with different boards.

Later USA editions were published by the Popular Library in 1967 (see page 45), and by Pyramid in 1973 (see page 46).

In 1969, Coward McCann published sections from *Sister of the Angels* in *The Ten Gifts* (see page 47), which also had selections from *Gentian Hill*, *White Witch*, *Bird in the Tree*, *Dean's Watch*, *Green Dolphin Street*, *Island Magic*, *Rosemary Tree*, *Pilgrim's Inn*, *Scent of Water*, *Heart of the Family*, and *Make Believe*—American titles given.

There were two separate French editions, both issued by Plon, the first in 1951, with a plain wrapper and another issued in 1953 with a wrapper in colour (see pages 48 and 49). The illustrations were by Françoise Estachy and the book was translated by Yvonne Girault.

There were also two German editions (see pages 50 and 51), the first published by Steinberg in Switzerland in 1957, and the second published in Germany by Herder in 1962. These editions were translated by Ursula von Wiese and illustrated with woodcuts (*Holzschnitte*) by Axel Leskoschek.

Girls Gone By first published *Sister of the Angels* in 2014, with an introduction by myself and a short history of Elizabeth Goudge by Ann Mackie-Hunter. We have not included these in this new edition but are delighted to have new introductions by John Gough and Mia Jha.

With apologies that some of the illustrations are not of good quality—they are the best I could find. And thank you to those who supplied replacements.

Clarissa Cridland

POPULAR LIBRARY EDITION, 1967

PYRAMID EDITION, 1973

ELIZABETH GOUDGE

La Sœur
DES ANGES
●
Le petit
CHEVAL
BLANC

PLON

10ᵉ mille

ELIZABETH GOUDGE

LA SOEUR des ANGES

PLON

Illustrations de
FRANÇOISE ESTAC

THE BOTTOM IS VERY SLIGHTLY CROPPED FROM THIS PICTURE BUT IT IS
MUCH THE BEST I HAVE FOUND.

THE SWISS-GERMAN EDITION

THE GERMAN EDITION

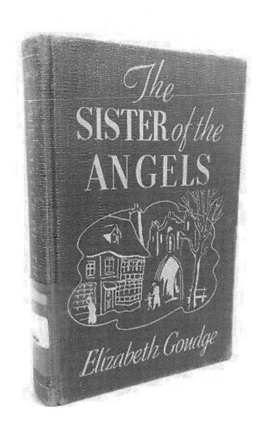

THE BOARDS OF THE AMERICAN EDITION REFERRED TO ON PAGE 42

NOTE ON THE TEXT

This GGBP edition of *Sister of the Angels* uses the text of the 1947 reprint; it contained very few errors, and we explain below how we have dealt with them. In accordance with our usual policy, we have not edited or updated the text in any way; we have, however, supplied one missing closing quotation mark at the end of a speech. Following that same policy, we have not changed two errors in case they are not typos but Elizabeth Goudge's own preference: Nicolas Broadbent's name for Henrietta, 'Suora Angelico', to match hers for him of 'Fra Angelico', should strictly be 'Suor Angelica', and on page 148 the verses of the carol should begin with 'O', not 'Oh'. The statement 'Grandfather and Hugh Anthony must have worked like blacks' (p138) would not appear in the work of a contemporary writer, but we have not changed it (see also John Gough's discussion of this point on p21).

We have standardised on the spelling 'Nicolas' for both the characters of that name, Broadbent and de Malden. 'Nicholas' occurred three times in Chapter III, twice for de Malden and once for Broadbent, but we believe these were simply mistakes by the original typesetter. We have corrected one occurrence of 'Hugh Antony' to the usual 'Hugh Anthony'. We have also corrected one obviously misspelt word, 'deficiences', to 'deficiencies'. On page 62 it is possible that 'Canon's gardens' should be 'Canons' gardens', but as we have no way of knowing we have left it.

On page 87 the original text reads: 'It did not seem possibly that one man could have done what Nicolas Broadbent had done.'

We have amended 'possibly' to 'possible'. On page 92 where the original says that Henrietta 'leapt upright as though somebody had suddenly tweaked her upwards up the hair' we have substituted 'by' for 'up'. On page 125 the 'a' is missing from the sentence 'She was not a scrap.' However, there is a gap of the right size in the printed page where it should have been, so it is clear that it was simply lost at the typesetting stage.

The original contained a few inconsistencies in the use of hyphens. Where we could identify a majority usage we have standardised on it, and we have thus amended one 'thank-you' to 'thank you', one 'drawing-paper' to 'drawing paper' and one 'good night' to 'good-night'. However, 'rose-colour'/'rose colour', 'nonplussed'/'non-plussed' and 'ticket collector'/'ticket-collector' all occurred once in each form, so we have left them unaltered.

Laura Hicks and Sarah Woodall

SISTER OF THE ANGELS

A CHRISTMAS STORY

BY

ELIZABETH GOUDGE

Illustrated by
C. WALTER HODGES

For those who love Henrietta

CONTENTS

Chapter I

The moment she woke up Henrietta was conscious that she was happy, unusually, deliciously happy. She opened her eyes, smiled, then shut them again, so that the outside world should not distract her mind as it gloated over her joy. She had three causes for it; the first snow of the year was lying thick and white over the world, it was a month to Christmas, and to-day her father was coming on a long visit.

The last cause for joy was the greatest, of course, for Henrietta adored her father. Thinking of him her lovely little mouth tilted up at the corners and her arms moved under the bedclothes ... Already she could see him coming, tall and thin, dark-haired and white-faced like herself, smiling at her, and already she was running to meet him with arms stretched out ... There was no one like him in all the world, she thought.

There certainly was not. Gabriel Ferranti was a name known now over a good part of the world. His genius as a writer was only matched by his genius in escaping responsibility. He slithered from beneath it with the expertness of a duck taking to the water. In his own element, the world of art, he floated supreme and confident, but when towed to and forced upon the dry land of practical affairs, when told, for instance, to turn his attention to the expenses of his small motherless daughter's education, he became hopelessly clumsy and incompetent: he quacked in horror and took to the water.

But Henrietta at eleven years old was untroubled by Ferranti's deficiencies as a parent. She saw nothing odd in the fact that he had been so vague and bungling a father that old Canon and Mrs. Fordyce had adopted her and taken her to live with them in the Cathedral Close of Torminster. She thought of him always as a fairy-tale figure, a sort of Pied-Piper of a man. His eccentric comings and goings in her life were quite in character and she did not worry about them.

She was right not to worry. He loved her. However far he had wandered across the world the thought of her and of Torminster brought him back to them at certain seasons: in the spring when the snowdrops, as white and dainty as Henrietta herself, were pushing up through the brown earth: in summer when the scent of roses drifted over the walls of the Canon's gardens and Henrietta went running through the streets of the old city in her pink frock, jumping and skipping because she was so happy; in autumn when the elm trees on the Cathedral Green dropped their leaves in a silent drifting shower of gold; and in December when Torminster lay hushed and still under a cold crystal sky and the Christmas bells rang out over the snow. At these times he came back and found his Henrietta waiting for him with a constant heart.

She was an enchanting creature; like a jasmine flower. She had the same grace and the same starry quality. Her sensitiveness and her sympathy were too quick and too keen for so young a child; they strained her body a little, so that she looked always too fine-drawn and too fragile for the world in which she found herself, her body a very thin shell for the burning leaping flame that was her spirit.

The setting of her room, white, austere, and with little cherubs carved in white stone set under the cornice, because this was a very old house that had once been part of a monastery, was just right for her. It had the same look of innocence, the same air of simplicity and attentive quiet. The snow-light that filled it suited them both; it was so crystal clear, so frail and lovely.

But cold. Henrietta, opening her eyes again, nipped her nose between finger and thumb and was slightly relieved to find it was not frost-bitten. "But I expect it's very pink," she thought, and looked up at the carved cherubs to see if theirs were pink … Poor little creatures, they had nothing on but wings, not even nightgowns … They were certainly pink, but not with cold; the dawn was flooding the world out of a clear sky, and the white room, and the white world outside the window, glowed with a sudden flowering of fragile colour.

"Only a month to Christmas!" sang Henrietta. "Only a month!" And suddenly she shot out of bed, for she still had so much to do. Grandmother's cross-stitch tea-cosy was only just begun, the silk tie she was going to knit for her father wasn't even started and she didn't know what she was going to make for Grandfather and Hugh Anthony, the other little orphan grandchild who lived with Grandmother and Grandfather, no real relation to her but the brother of her heart. "I've everything to do!" she cried. Yet she was pleased about it. She liked being busy.

But it was cold in that room with nothing on but a nightgown. It was the beginning of the century and central heating was unknown: nor would Grandmother have allowed it in a bedroom even had it been known, for she disapproved very strongly of what she called "coddling." Grandfather was allowed a fire, a small one, in his study all day long because it is well known that clergymen cannot write good sermons if their feet are cold, and there was an oil stove in the dining-room and a fire in the drawing-room in the afternoons only. But that was all. A fire in one's bedroom, unless one was very ill indeed, was not allowed, however many degrees below zero the thermometer might have fallen ... Though guests might have the oil stove in the spare room if they were delicate and had a cold threatening, and it was remarkable how often colds did threaten when they came to stay with the Fordyces.

Henrietta, considering the brass can of warm water that Sarah had placed in her basin while she was still asleep, wrestled with her conscience. In this cold weather she and Hugh Anthony had their twice-weekly baths in tin tubs before the kitchen fire, bathrooms being as yet unknown in Torminster, but on other days they were expected to wash all over, in their rooms, "by bits." It was a process that called for real skill. The technical problem was how to wash a square foot of back, for instance, without uncovering the rest of yourself to the icy air, and it was difficult to solve, but the moral problem was much worse; was it compatible with the Christian religion, which commands its devotees to "endure hardness," to skimp washing on the very iciest of the cold days? Henrietta thought that it was, but found it very hard to decide what days could truthfully be described as the "very iciest," and what portions of the body might be left out upon them.

"It is 'very iciest' to-day," said Henrietta's lower nature.

"No," said her conscience.

"Almost 'very iciest'."

"No."

"But cold. Cold enough only to have to do my top."

"Down to the waist."

"Not quite down to the waist. If I went down to the waist that would be middle, and I'm not doing middle."

"If you shirk your middle this morning you must do it to-night."

"Of course," said Henrietta's lower nature rather arrogantly. "But I shan't do my legs at all to-day, not whatever you say I shan't."

Her conscience said a good deal more but she paid no attention to it. She wriggled her nightgown off her shoulders, gritted her teeth and squeezed out the sponge.

But within the limits agreed upon she did the job very thoroughly, so thoroughly that by the time she had dressed herself in her scarlet jersey and dark-blue skirt, brushed and plaited her long dark hair and stripped her bed neatly, she was glowing all over with self-righteousness and wondering how much washing Hugh Anthony had done. As his elder by a year she felt it her duty to go and see.

But Hugh Anthony had already gone down stairs, leaving his little room as though wrecked by an earthquake. She stripped his bed, folded his pyjamas, restored the contents of his drawers, strewn on the floor, to their proper places, said a polite good-morning to his two white mice, Hengist and Horsa, and was about to leave the room when something in their expressions made her turn back and look at the water in his basin ... It was of a most unusual clarity.

"How much did he wash?" she asked the white mice.

They said nothing but looked very sad.

"Not even his teeth?" she asked. "Nothing?"

They still made no remarks and turned their backs so that only their depressed tails could be seen. Henrietta raced from the room, swung herself astride the wide banisters, slid down them, sprang across the old stone hall and into the dining-room, where Hugh Anthony lay beside the stove on his front, *The Times* spread out on the floor before him, reading it in the only comfortable position in which perusal of that awkwardly-shaped journal is at all possible.

"Hugh Anthony," said Henrietta, "you've not washed."

"I have," said Hugh Anthony.

"Liar! You haven't."

"Liar yourself," said Hugh Anthony pleasantly. "I have."

"What did you wash?"

"Hengist and Horsa."

"But Hengist and Horsa aren't part of you."

"They are. They're mine and I love them, and what you love is part of you. Grandfather said so."

"Well, I don't think it's true love to wash people when they don't like being washed. Not in this weather."

"It was only their tails," said Hugh Anthony. "Here, look at this!"

The mice forgotten, Henrietta flopped to her front beside Hugh Anthony. With her elbows on the floor, her chin propped in her hands and her long thin legs kicking in the air, she read in the agony column where Hugh Anthony's stubby forefinger directed. They were both inveterate readers of the agony column. It suggested to them endless exciting stories; murders, burglaries, thrills of all sorts. It was almost better than Sherlock Holmes because it left more to the imagination.

The present paragraph requested that John Henry Barnes, last heard of a year ago when he left Dartmoor after serving a term of imprisonment, should communicate with a certain lawyer's office in London, where he would learn something greatly to his advantage.

"I expect he's been left a fortune," said Hugh Anthony excitedly. "I expect he murdered somebody nasty and the relatives were so grateful that they've all subscribed."

"If he did," said Henrietta, "I'm sure it was entirely by accident. I'm sure he's a nice man. He's been left a gold mine, I shouldn't wonder. Let's tell a story about it. You begin."

"Once upon a time," said Hugh Anthony, kicking his legs, and rambled off into a highly-coloured account of the mine, his voice growing huskier and huskier and more and more impressive as he warmed to it. He was a good story-teller. Ignorance of his subject merely lent wings to his imagination, and probability was not a thing that he took into account at all. Henrietta, enthralled, wriggled nearer to him, until her smooth dark head was pressed close against his flaming curly red one and her kicking legs were entwined with his. They seemed one child then, bound together in the glorious thrill of make-believe.

Yet another part of Henrietta, that curious second self whom we seem to carry about with us, that self that criticizes, observes and admonishes, was all the time not attending to Hugh Anthony's story. It was seeing a waste of snow and a grim prison upon a moor. It was seeing a lonely figure pushed out of that prison and set free upon the moor; but with nowhere to go, nothing to do, no money, no friends, no food. It was seeing that figure wandering up and down the world for a whole year, still with nothing to do, nowhere to go. And now it was nearly Christmas again, and snowing again. Where did the homeless go at Christmas? Who looked after them? And did they ever read the newspapers?

"What's the matter, Henrietta?" asked Hugh Anthony suddenly. "You're shivering. And you're not attending either."

"I am! I am!" cried Henrietta. "Go on about them blowing the gold out of the rock with gunpowder." And she wriggled yet closer to him, smacking her other self firmly upon the head and trying to fix her whole attention upon that cavern of Hugh Anthony's, lit by sparkling gleams of gunpowder that exploded as quietly and harmlessly as fireworks on the fifth of November, letting out streams of liquid gold that flowed from the rock like beer from the cask when the tap is turned. She succeeded this time. The story gripped her utterly and that figure on the moor was quite forgotten.

It was so that Grandfather, entering with the morning post, found them, lying together in the glow of the stove, illumined by the snow-light, their faces bright with their dreams. He polished his glasses that he might see them better, for they looked adorable; the one so black and white, so fragile and starry, the other so sturdy, so snub-nosed, so freckled and so glowing. He would not have disturbed them, not for the world, but the entrance of Sarah the elderly parlourmaid with fried sausages, followed by Grandmother carrying the silver tea-caddy that no one but herself might touch, put an abrupt end to all voyagings of the spirit. In one bound the children were in their places at the table, standing with bowed heads for Grandfather to say grace.

"For what we are about to receive," murmured Grandfather, "may the Lord make us ... Now, Hugh Anthony, you sat down to sausage before I had finished. That was very wrong, very un-Christian. I shall now have to say grace all over again. Stand up."

Hugh Anthony stood up and Grandfather began again. "For what we are about to receive may the Lord make us truly thankful. Amen."

It was Henrietta who sat down first this time, and Grandfather feared that the sound of his Amen had not quite died away before her body was in swift descent. But he overlooked it. She was a little excited. She had been given a few days' holiday from school because her father was coming.

"A letter from your father," he said, smiling at her. "Telling us the time of his train, no doubt."

Henrietta jigged up and down in her seat. "It'll be the morning one," she said. "The 12.15. He's coming from Medwell, not from London, so it'll be the 12.15. Say it's the 12.15!"

"12.15," corroborated Grandfather.

"And I may meet him?" asked Henrietta. "I may meet him by myself?"

"It would be a sheer waste of your time, dear," said Grandmother. "I've never known that man catch any train he said he'd catch. Incapable of it. Artistic." She sniffed in some indignation, for Gabriel Ferranti was no favourite of hers, and turned her attention to the ritual of tea-making.

But Grandfather, who loved Ferranti, turned to the crestfallen Henrietta with a comforting smile. "He'll be there, Henrietta. Getting near Christmas and his daughter to meet him. I told him you'd meet him. He'll not fail you."

Henrietta smiled and was happy.

"Grandmother, may I have another sausage?" asked Hugh Anthony.

"Certainly not," said Grandmother.

"Why?" asked Hugh Anthony.

"Because you've had two already."

"But why can't I have three?"

"Because three wouldn't be good for you."

"Why?"

"Because they are made of pork, and too much pork is not good for children."

"They aren't made of pork. Sarah says Mr. King's sausages are made of horse. So may I have another?"

"No, Hugh Anthony."

"Why not?"

"I've already told you why not."

"But you haven't, Grandmother. You said because pork, and I say not pork, horse. And horse is very digestible; starving people eat it and don't die. So may I?"

"That will do, Hugh Anthony."

"Why?"

Grandfather leaned sideways beyond the bowl of ferns and cut geraniums that separated him from Grandmother, so that his pleading blue eyes, so startlingly young in his old face and above his white beard, could meet hers. "There is a very little sausage in the dish, dear. Quite a small one. And I think the dear boy is hungry. It's a cold day. Very cold."

"Very well, Theobald," said Grandmother. "Have it your own way. If these children's characters are ruined, don't blame me." And with her black eyes snapping indignantly in her wrinkled little face, and her grey cork-screw curls quivering beneath her lace cap, she erected the tea-cosy between herself and her aggravating family. She feared for the future of these grandchildren of hers. She doubted if their characters were being sufficiently disciplined. Left to herself, eighty-two years old though she was, she could have done it with the assistance of a slipper, corners, and plenty of bed-with-no-supper: but Grandfather, though only eighty, was as hopelessly lenient as an old man of ninety; he could never seem to lay his hand on a slipper just when it was wanted, corners were abhorrent to him, and if she prescribed bed-with-no-supper he was sure to slip up the back stairs with a couple of peppermint drops hidden in an envelope and a banana protruding from his tail coat pocket ... She sighed and turned her attention to the business of the day. Grandfather was Canon-in-residence this month and that meant, for her, the Cathedral flowers to see to.

"There's that christening, this afternoon," she informed her family. "The choirman's baby. A nice little thing, though I think it has adenoids. I've got white chrysanthemums for the font. The children can take them down after breakfast. And on your way to the station, Henrietta, you can get me two and sixpence worth of half-penny stamps for my Christmas cards. You'd better go to the Cathedral, too, Theobald, and see that Hugh Anthony goes on to school and Henrietta arranges those chrysanthemums properly. She's inclined to be too exuberant with flowers."

She was. She adored flowers. At the thought of arranging them for a baby's christening she wriggled ecstatically in her chair and swallowed the rest of her breakfast in a way that would be bound to cause indigestion later.

"Now! Now!" she cried to Grandfather and Hugh Anthony when she had finished, and raced upstairs to put on her new red reefer coat, her gaiters and her scarlet cap.

When she came down again she found that there was a bit of bother going on in the hall.

"I won't go to school in gaiters," said Hugh Anthony to his grandparents, and took up a Napoleonic position; legs wide apart, head thrown back, hands clasped in the small of the back.

Grandfather, Grandmother and Henrietta sighed. They were busy enough in all conscience, what with one thing and another, without Hugh Anthony being taken with one of his "difficult" moods and taking up their time with the subduing of it.

"Only babies wear gaiters," said Hugh Anthony. "I'm ten. I ought to be wearing trousers."

"You ought not," said Grandmother. "When you are eleven and go to boarding school you will wear trousers, but while you merely go to this little day school you will keep to your knicker-bockers and socks, with gaiters in cold weather. There they are. Put them on."

"I won't," said Hugh Anthony. "And why must I still go to day school? Everybody says it's high time I went to boarding school. Why can't I go to boarding school?"

"We cannot afford it at present," said Grandmother. "If your grandfather hadn't given away that legacy to persons unknown we might have thought of it for you this year, but as things are you must wait till next year. Put on your gaiters."

Poor Grandfather looked dreadfully uncomfortable. He had been left a small legacy by a relative, something to do with a gold mine, and had put it at the disposal of a person or persons whose need, he said, was greater than his. Grandmother was annoyed about it for she considered that charity should begin at home. She would have found that legacy very useful; she wanted new curtains in the drawing-room as well as boarding school for her ebullient grandson. Moreover Grandfather did not tell her who the needy unknown was, so that her curiosity as well as her need remained unsatisfied. She sighed.

"Look at Henrietta in her gaiters," said Grandfather, hastily changing the conversation. "How nice she looks."

"She's only a woman," said Hugh Anthony scornfully. "Women! They're babies till they die."

"Horrid little boy!" flashed Henrietta, scarlet with indignation.

"That'll do," said Grandmother. "The snow is on the ground, the wind is in the north, and no un-gaitered children leave this house to-day."

"Well, Henrietta," sighed Grandfather, "we'll have to go without him. A pity! A sad pity!" And he wound his muffler round his throat, spreading his white beard carefully out over it, poised his round clerical hat on his bald head and prepared to leave with Henrietta.

Hugh Anthony protruded his lower lip and pondered. Going out with the others, and then on to school, would be fun, while staying in with Grandmother would not, but on the other hand it was out of the question that the flag of his pride should be lowered and his will beaten down by a couple of women and an old man. He thought hard and fast and the idea of a compromise suggested itself to him as desirable. He sat down abruptly upon the hall chair, folded his arms across his chest and extended his sturdy legs stiffly in front of him.

Henrietta was quick to take the hint. She seized the gaiters, sank to her knees and hastily fitted those articles of apparel into position, working the buttonhook with lightning speed and keeping one elbow firmly planted upon Hugh Anthony's middle lest he should change his mind and dash off. But Hugh Anthony was quite satisfied with the turn of events. He had uttered no word of apology or yielding, he had reduced Henrietta to an attitude of humility suited to her sex, and he was going out. He smiled a fat smile and intimated to his Grandfather that he might hand him his scarlet woollen gloves from off the hall table.

Chapter II

Outside in the street, carrying the lovely chrysanthemums that Grandmother grew in the greenhouse to the glory of God and because it was cheaper to grow flowers for the floral decorations than to buy them, they felt very happy.

The Cathedral city of Torminster looked very lovely under its mantle of snow. Though it was built in the valley it seemed suddenly to have become, thought Henrietta, a city in the mountains. The slanting, snow-covered roofs, all of different heights and shapes, belonging to houses that had grown up like flowers one by one through the centuries, looked like tumbled mountain slopes, and the cold keen air was like the rarefied air one breathes high up in the sky. The sun was bright in a dome of blue crystal and the shadows were violet-tinted like the shadows in mountain crevasses.

But the crowning glory was the Cathedral itself. It rose up like some great enchanted mountain, its three towers soaring up into the sky as though they did not mean to stop until they had pierced the crystal dome and come face to face with the rainbow encircled throne that was built above it. Every ledge and pinnacle, every carved angel and saint and demon, was outlined with frosted snow, and the Virgin and Child over the west door were so covered with it that it looked as though an armful of Christmas roses had been dropped over them, the blossoms lodging in the folds of the Virgin's robe and the outstretched hands of the Child.

"I wish we could bring him inside," said Henrietta, worried. "I'm afraid he'll catch cold out there."

She had once seen, or thought she had seen, the carved Child laugh and clap his hands, and ever since then she could not get it out of her head that he was real.

"Look," said Grandfather comfortingly, "he is inside too."

They were standing just inside the west door, she and Grandfather, for Hugh Anthony had gone off to school, and looking up the length of the great nave they could see the second statue of the Virgin and Child that stood high up in the inverted arch that supported the central tower. It was so far away that on many days, gilded though it was, it was almost lost in the darkness, but to-day a shaft of sunlight, shining through a clerestory window, lit it up with such a golden glory that it seemed like a lamp shining in the heart of the shadowy Cathedral, lighting up a little and no more of this

75

mysterious great building that man had built to the glory of God.

Henrietta suddenly caught her breath. Always it seemed to her quite incredible that men could have made this place; people like herself and Hugh Anthony only bigger; how could they have done it? She looked about her. The massive pillars of the nave were so tall that they seemed to be lifting up the soaring arches they carried far out of sight, while below them the aisles stretched away unendingly into shadowed space. The sunshine came through the stained glass windows curiously changed, split up into reds and blues and greens, robbed of its brightness and subdued to the colours of mystery. Everywhere was this sense of space and height and a reaching out to an end that was never found. There was no time here. Past and present and future were all one.

Henrietta had an unaccustomed feeling of panic. The place in its eternal greatness and grandeur seemed to her as frightening as life itself ... Although she was only eleven she knew that some people found life very frightening, and as a matter of fact it hadn't been very nice to her before she came to live with Grandfather and Grandmother ... Here she was, a little midge of a thing, alive whether she liked it or not, gripped by life as she was gripped by this great Cathedral. Hardly knowing what she did, driven by an instinct of escape, she slipped her hand out of Grandfather's and turned back towards the wide open west door, where outside the sunshine blazed.

And as she did so she saw a figure flash suddenly out of the sunshine and stand in the doorway. He did not seem to have walked there, he seemed suddenly to have appeared. The dazzle of the sun behind him made it impossible for her to distinguish either his face or his clothes; he was just an immensely tall black figure, man himself, appearing out of nowhere and entering the dark house of life. She thought of the figure of the man lost on the moor that she had seen in her imagination; she thought of it and for no reason at all her throat hurt her.

"Come, Henrietta. Here's Peppercorn with the water."

Henrietta suddenly came to herself to find Grandfather with his hand on her shoulder and kind Peppercorn, the head verger, beaming down at her through his spectacles. She gave herself a little shake and turned her attention to floral decoration.

This usually made her blissfully happy, but to-day, somehow, it didn't. She hoped the poor little adenoidal baby who was going to be christened was going to enjoy being alive; she hoped so, but she couldn't feel sure. She kept thinking of that man on the moor, and of the dark figure in the doorway. She had to keep reminding herself that over the doorway of the Cathedral, at the threshold of the house of life, was the Child holding out his arms in welcome; and that inside he was here, too, far up in the roof, lit by the sunshine … But so far away, so difficult to get to.

"Don't be silly, Henrietta," she said to herself. "You bolted your breakfast."

But when their work was finished she found that she did not want to go home with Grandfather, she wanted to stay by herself in the Cathedral until it was time to go and meet her father. Her fear of the Cathedral had been only momentary. It was once more her friend whose beauty comforted her in all the puzzles of her growing mind.

"Could I stay, Grandfather?" she asked.

"Certainly, dear," said Grandfather.

She stood on tiptoe, reaching up to whisper to him. "Could I have the key of the chapel of Nicolas de Malden?"

Grandfather's eyes popped slightly in astonishment, and he hesitated. The chapel of Nicolas de Malden was a very precious chapel down in the crypt. It was always kept locked up so that wicked tourists should not scratch their names on the glorious frescos that adorned its walls, but all the Canons had a key of it.

"What for?" asked Grandfather.

"There are some flowers left," said Henrietta. "I'd like to put them there."

"But it's Advent," protested Grandfather. "We don't put flowers in the chapels in Advent."

Henrietta shrugged with sudden impatience. This ridiculous notion of not having flowers in Advent and Lent annoyed her. There should be flowers in God's house always ... God's house. The house of life. Which was it? Both? ... Well, anyway, there should be flowers in it. Her lips closed in a firm line and she held out her hand for the key.

Obediently Grandfather took out his key-ring. There were times when Henrietta could be exceedingly obstinate, and at these times nobody, not even Grandfather, could get the better of her. This was apparently one of those times. He handed her the key and turned away. "But remember," he cautioned, "to lock the door when you come away and bring the key with you. Don't forget, Henrietta."

"Of course not," said Henrietta, and stuck her chin in the air rather naughtily. As if she'd forget a thing like that, and she eleven!

She gathered the left-over chrysanthemums together in a bunch and made her way up the nave with her nose buried in their cool aromatic softness. There was a cupboard full of vases down in the crypt, and a tap of water. She would have a good time arranging them ... And she would have an even better time when Christmas came and every one of the chapels and chantries had to be decorated with flowers and holly berries ... Thinking about it she paused to look at a chantry she particularly loved, where the carved figure of a knight lay sleeping, his feet propped against his dog. Henrietta loved that dog. She would make him a collar of holly berries for Christmas.

"Still frightened?" asked a voice.

She started and looked up. There were, even in this weather, several visitors moving, singly or in groups, round the Cathedral, for Torminster Cathedral was one of the glories of the west country and even in winter people came to see it. One of these, a tall, grey-haired, hungry-looking man, was standing beside Henrietta, looking

amusedly down at her. She knew instantly that he was the man she had seen standing in the Cathedral door, and she looked at him eagerly. He was not an old man, in spite of his grey hair, for he held himself very erect and the eyes in his weather-beaten face were of an unusually bright and fiery blue. His clothes were disreputable and his shoes worn through, yet he was well-shaven and his hands were clean. How did he know she had been frightened?

"I saw you as I came in," he said, smiling. "I felt as you did the first time I came into this place … Do you like that dog?" And he nodded towards the carved dog in the chantry. He had a queer voice, husky and very slow, as though he wasn't used to talking a great deal.

"He is my very particular friend," said Henrietta in her clear sweet treble. "His name is Eric. I would tell you all about him, only it happens that I am a little pressed for time just now. But perhaps some other day, if you are staying in Torminster, you would like me to tell you about him."

She spoke with exquisite politeness and friendliness, although with a graciousness that was a little shattering, issuing from so small a person. She was naturally friendly and Grandfather had trained her to be very courteous to Cathedral visitors, no matter how tiresome they might be. They were the guests of the Cathedral and all possible information and assistance should be offered them.

"Thank you," said the stranger with becoming humility. "I am only passing through Torminster, so I am afraid I must remain in ignorance of Eric's no doubt most interesting history. I would not, of course, dream of detaining you now." And he bowed to her with a bow that seemed a little awkward, as though, like his voice, it had not been used much lately. Henrietta rather thought that he was wanting to detain her, but with the flowers to do and then her father to meet she really couldn't stop. So she bowed graciously and passed on.

Down in the damp close darkness of the crypt she found her vase, filled it with water and carried it to a heavy oak door hidden in the shadows. She unlocked it, leaving the key in the lock, and went in, closing the door behind her. She was now in pitch darkness, but she knew just where the matches were kept, behind a stone to the right of the door. She set down her flowers, struck a match and made her way to the altar, where she lit the candles in the great branched candlesticks that stood there. The flames of them burned up straight and splendid, for the chapel was window-less and no draughts stirred its still air. They showed the chapel of Nicolas de Malden in all its glory.

It was very small and looked as though it were hewn out of

the solid rock, like a catacomb chapel. Three of the walls and the concave roof were covered with the most amazing medieval frescos, marvellously restored by a modern craftsman whose genius could have been no less than that of the original artist. Overhead were the courts of heaven, with the angels, archangels, saints and martyrs gathered round the crowned Christ upon his throne, and on the west, north and south walls was depicted a crowding, jostling, panic-stricken throng of men and women and demons upon the judgment day. The genius of the two painters took away the breath of any one who came into the chapel. The first man had known little about perspective, and less about the anatomy of the human figure, and his successor had not tried to minimize his ignorance but had contented himself with revealing afresh in that tiny chapel the glory of heaven, the terror of hell and all the joy and despair and triumph and hatred of humanity upon the day of judgment. Upon some of the faces of the men and demons one could not look for horror, but from the face of the Christ one could not take one's eyes. And the colouring was most lovely, clear and fresh, blue and green and gold, with rose colour in the angels' wings and scarlet and amethyst bordering the robes of the saints. There was very little furniture in the chapel, only a rough stone altar with a cross and the candlesticks upon it, and a bench against the west wall.

But upon the east wall, behind the altar, the frescos had not been finished; had hardly even been begun. There were only a few vague outlines to show where the medieval artist had begun to block out his figures, only a faint wash of blue and rose-colour to indicate the colour scheme that he had wanted, and these so obscured by time that there was no guessing what scene he had had in mind. Privileged people who were shown the chapel, but not told the story of it, guessed that here the old painter's intention had baffled the modern artist; unable to guess at it he had left well alone.

But Henrietta, who had heard something of the tragic story of the chapel of Nicolas de Malden, knew why it was that that east wall was unfinished. As she put her vase of chrysanthemums upon the altar she told herself what she knew of the history all over again, both parts of it, the story of the first artist and the story of the second artist, and even though the first part had happened centuries ago, and the second part years before she had come to live at Torminster, it made her, as always, feel unhappy. She could never feel, as people told her she should feel, that because a particular bit of history was over and done with that it did not matter any more. She had a feeling that no story ever was over and done with; not unless it came full circle round again and the intention of it was completed ... And the chapel of Nicolas de Malden was not completed.

Chapter III

This Nicolas de Malden had been a monk in the old monastery that had been built centuries ago beside the Cathedral. He had been an artist, and the greatest missal painter of his time, famous all over Europe for the glory of his art. But he was not a selfish artist, to shut himself up with paints and brushes and take no heed of the world outside his cell. He laboured among the poor more fervently than any of the other monks, and he had no fear, for he would enter the most terrible hovels and would bind up the sores of the lepers with his own hands. But the fates were jealous, it seemed, for one day as he stood before the high altar, assisting the abbot in the celebration of the mass, he saw upon his hands the marks of leprosy.

So then he knew himself to be an outcast; a tainted creature who might never again talk with his fellow men, or eat with them, or rejoice with them in the light of the sun. But he would not go and live at the leper hospital in the city; instead he went down to the crypt and told the sorrowing monks that he would live there by himself until he died.

For the first three days the monk who every morning brought him food and water, and rush lights in iron holders to lighten the long hours of the night, saw him sitting desolately in a dark corner, brooding, and he was very sad, but on the fourth day he saw to his delight that Brother Nicolas was busying himself about something. He had gone into a little concave window-less stone cell in the corner of the crypt, where gardening tools and such oddments were kept, and was nosing about in there like a dog at a rabbit hole. He called out that the visiting monk should go and fetch him water, a scrubbing brush, a small ladder, paints and other necessities for tempera painting.

From that day on the monk who came to him daily always found him busy in the little concave cell, working by the light of innumerable rushlights, but he did not dare to come too close and see what he was doing lest he should catch the leprosy. It seemed that for a long time his disease spared Brother Nicolas's hands, but the day came when the visiting monk found him painting with the brush held between his teeth. Then it seemed that either the painting was finished, or else Brother Nicolas could do no more, for the monk found him painfully rolling the loose stones that lay about the crypt inside the building, for what purpose he did not know.

But one day when he came with the bread and water and called out in greeting, there was no answer, though light was burning in the little cell. Greatly daring he tiptoed to the door and looked in. All over the ceiling and three of the walls spread a glory of colour such as his eyes had never seen, a pictured heaven and earth and hell upon the judgment day, with its apex a painted Christ from whose stern yet pitiful face the monk could not take his eyes. To the east was a rough stone altar made of piled stones, with rushlights burning upon it, and before the altar, facing the unfinished east wall and crouched on the floor as though he had fallen forward while he prayed, was the dead body of Nicolas de Malden.

As long as the monastery lasted Nicolas de Malden was revered as a saint, the chapel was lovingly cared for and a service was held there every Christmas Eve in his honour and that of the other Saint Nicolas, the Christmas saint. Then the time came when bluff King Hal destroyed the monastery and the monks fled; but before they went, fearing the desecration of their shrine, they blocked up its door.

The years went by and the story of Nicolas de Malden, that had never been set down in writing, was yet handed down from father to son and lived on. But only as a legend. No one really believed that that chapel existed.

And then Grandfather came to Torminster, heard the legend and was fascinated by it. "Always a foundation of truth in these tales," he said, and went ferreting about in the crypt until he found what looked like a blocked-up door. "We will take it down," he said gently but firmly to the Dean and the other Canons. "Waste of time," they said. "Take it down," persisted Grandfather, and he went on persisting so long and so monotonously that at last in sheer self-defence they gave in. "But you'll see," they said, "there'll be nothing there but dead bats and dirt."

And at first sight it seemed that they were right, for a scene of desolation met the eyes of the workmen who unblocked the door. Part of the roof had fallen in, the walls were disfigured with damp, and rubbish was piled on the floor. The Dean and the other Canons remarked happily that this was only what they had expected and were a little disconcerted when further examination revealed the traces of disfigured, almost obliterated frescos to their unbelieving gaze; but cheered up again to point out to the jubilant Grandfather how impossible it would be to get the fallen stones back into place or to restore the paintings.

"Nonsense," said Grandfather. "Under the guidance of God it will be done."

And it so happened that just at this time Peppercorn took a party of tourists round the Cathedral and among them was a young architect and artist, Nicolas Broadbent, who arrogantly declared that he could restore the chapel to its original glory ... And Grandfather felt guided to take him round to the Deanery at nine o'clock in the evening, when the Dean had been mellowed by his nightly glass of port, and let him talk the old man into agreement. The other

Canons were outraged. They had never heard of Nicolas Broadbent, therefore he could be of no use. He was probably an unscrupulous scoundrel. What were his qualifications, they asked Grandfather. "His name," said Grandfather, "is Nicolas; and from what I have seen of his art I like it."

The second Nicolas, like the first, provided himself with all the necessities for his work and shut himself up in the crypt. He knew a good deal about building, as well as about painting, and he would allow no one to help him or see what he was doing except a couple of stone-masons and the carpenter who was making the strong oak door to protect the Chapel. Like the first Nicolas he had his meals brought to him in the crypt and only left it at night to get some sleep in the attic bedroom he had rented at Peppercorn's house.

At last the day came when he sent for the Dean and Canons to see what he had done. He had not tackled the east wall yet, he said, but that would be finished in time for the dedication service on Christmas Eve. One by one they filed into the little chapel and stood staring. They could not speak. It did not seem possible that one man could have done what Nicolas Broadbent had done. Their eyes went from the painted figures of men and demons on the wall, restored to their original glory with an amazing genius, up to the saints and angels thronging the courts of heaven, and on to the face of the crowned Christ above, and there they stayed.

At last Grandfather turned to the young man beside him and looked at his scarred hands and haggard face. "Dear me," he said, "you'd better take a holiday, Nicolas."

"When I have done the east wall I will," said Nicolas.

But he never did the east wall. It was still untouched on Christmas Eve, when the service of re-dedication took place and the choir, singing gloriously, filed down from the nave to the dark crypt below; as they had done every Christmas Eve in the old days when the monastery still lived. Nicolas de Malden's chapel was filled with flowers and candles burned on the altar. There was a beautiful service, the choir standing outside in the crypt singing hymns and carols and the Dean and the Canons standing inside the chapel robed in their festival copes. But in the middle of the service Grandfather, who was reading a lesson, broke down and could not go on for a good five minutes; for Nicolas Broadbent had been arrested for forgery and put in prison; and he had loved the young man.

Everyone but Grandfather remarked that they had said all along that Nicolas was probably a scoundrel, and what a pity it was that they had not been listened to at the time, and what an appalling thing that owing to them not being listened to their beautiful Cathedral should have been desecrated by the hand of a forger. "But, if he is guilty, and it is not proved yet that he is, such a beautiful forger," murmured Grandfather. "They say those bank-notes brought tears of delight to the eyes of the experts." That made it no better, said Torminster. Grandfather said, yes, he thought it did, for if you were going to forge a bank note, a practice which of course he was not advocating or condoning for a single moment, surely it was better to forge one that was perfect of its kind than one that wasn't … Much better, said Torminster sarcastically, because then you would not be so likely to be caught. The Cathedral was desecrated, and that was that … It was not, said Grandfather; they must not confuse the forger with the artist; a man in his professional and private lives is often two different people and it was the artist, a fine and sincere artist too, who had put his mark upon Torminster Cathedral, and not the forger … Nicolas himself had apparently understood this for the name under which he had worked as architect and painter, Nicolas Broadbent, was not his real name … And anyhow, said Grandfather, would they kindly remember that Nicolas was not yet proved guilty of the charge, and if it should so fall out that judgment was given against him would they also kindly remember that whatever our sins there is good in all, and great good, he was sure, in Nicolas Broadbent. What good? asked Torminster. His motives had been excellent, said Grandfather. When he had first, as a very young man, strayed from the narrow way; if he *had* strayed from it, but they must remember that it wasn't proved yet: he had done it to win a livelihood for young scamps of brothers and sisters dependent on him. Yes, said Grandfather, this being his final word before going off to London to attend Nicolas's trial, come what might he believed there was great good in him.

It was Grandfather who paid for Nicolas's defence and Grandfather who, when the defence failed and Nicolas was sentenced to a long term of imprisonment, saw to it that the young scamps of brothers and sisters were cared for and set in the way of earning their own livings, and Grandfather who visited Nicolas in prison and insisted that Nicolas was to tell him the date of his release, so that he could meet him and put into execution a nice little plan that he had concocted for the future.

But Nicolas didn't tell him the date of his release. He just walked out of prison and disappeared and Grandfather's heart, that had been broken and mended again so many times in the course of his ministry that it was a wonder, at his age, that it held together at all, was broken all over again.

Chapter IV

Poor Grandfather!" murmured Henrietta, thinking over what she knew of this story as she set the vase of chrysanthemums upon the altar and slipped her fingers under the blossoms to lift them up to a fuller beauty. "It was selfish of Nicolas not to want to be helped. Selfish and proud. The first Nicolas would not have behaved like that." And then it struck her that perhaps the first Nicolas *had* behaved rather like that, for he had chosen to live and die by himself in the crypt rather than be properly looked after in the hospital ... Arrogant outcasts, both of them ... But she liked them, and felt they were her friends. "We *have* to let ourselves be looked after when it's necessary," she said severely, as though addressing them both. "It's naughty not to."

Then, her flowers arranged to her liking, she knelt down at the altar step, took a crumpled piece of paper from her pocket and spread it out on the floor before her.

It was her design for that unfinished east wall.

Other people, confronted with these vague outlines and blurs of colour, were utterly nonplussed. They couldn't imagine what the first Nicolas had had in mind to portray there. Henrietta, though of course she couldn't say so, thought they were a lot of duffers. *She* knew what he had had in mind. It was as clear as daylight to her. She had only to look at the east wall to see the picture blazing there; and the second Nicolas, she was sure, had seen the same picture, and would have painted it had they given him time.

There, where there was the hint of blue to the right, the Virgin was sitting, with the Child lying in a little wooden manger where, as in the legend, the hay had blossomed miraculously into flower petals. Behind her Joseph was standing; a tall cloaked figure leaning on a staff who stood like a great rock of protection between the Mother and the Child and the dangerous world beyond the stable. Through the half open door behind him one could see this world; storm-clouds lowering over snow-covered mountains, soldiers marching and wild beasts upon the prowl. To the left a deeper flush of colour upon the wall showed where the shepherds were kneeling with their offerings. The animals stood near the manger, of course, the ox and the ass, a black kitten and a little dog like Eric up in the chantry. And in the background, in the centre, two sweeping curved lines showed Henrietta where the Angel Gabriel stood, great wings radiating light and hands placed palm to palm upon his breast.

It was all so clear to Henrietta. If Nicolas de Malden had painted the second coming upon the other walls of course he would have painted the first coming upon this one. That, to her, was obvious. Nicolas would not have frightened people by portraying God the just and terrible judge unless at the same time he had comforted them with a picture of God the Child who himself endured the whole range of human suffering from birth to death.

"And let himself be looked after sometimes," said Henrietta with great firmness as though still addressing Nicolas the First and Nicolas the Second. And sitting back on her heels she produced a stumpy pencil, sucked it vigorously, though Grandfather had expressly told her that she must not suck pencils, and bent low over her drawing spread out upon the altar step. For she felt that she had not made this point sufficiently clear; she must stress the Child's dependence upon the father and mother who protected him and the friends who brought him needed gifts. With a few deft lines she raised Joseph's arm a little higher, made Mary's cloak sweep around the foot of the manger and added a little bottle of wine and a loaf of bread to the gifts that lay before it.

Undoubtedly Henrietta was an artist of no mean ability. As her father with his pen, and Grandfather through the medium of a dedicated life, so she with her pencil could portray the visions that she saw and give them to the world as her gift of gratitude for its nurture and its teaching ... Or would do one day, when her brush and pencil had been trained ... At present her pictures were a little confused, a little uncertain about perspective and anatomy, a little, in fact, like the pictures of the first Nicolas.

A slow, measured, booming sound made itself heard even down in the darkness of the crypt and Henrietta, who by this time was lying flat on her front on the chapel floor, lost in the glory of creation, leapt upright as though somebody had suddenly tweaked her upwards by the hair. Twelve o'clock striking! And her father due at the station at 12.15! In the excitement of her picture she had actually forgotten her adored, longed-for father.

"And the snow'll keep me from running fast!" she gasped as she dashed through the dark crypt and up the steps. "God!" she commanded, "let the snow make the train late ... Please," she added as an afterthought, and flew on down the nave.

But at the west door an awful thought struck her; in her hurry she had left the key of the chapel in the door; and after being so high and mighty with Grandfather about not forgetting it, too. "Just like me!" she sighed. "Just like me!" But she couldn't go back now. There wasn't time. She and Father must fetch the key on their way home from the station.

"But, God," she further commanded the Deity as she ran across the Cathedral Green towards the Market Place, "don't let any one go into the chapel and do any harm there. You won't, will you? Please!"

The Market Place looked lovely under the snow, but she hadn't time to stop; not even at the post office to get Grandmother's stamps. She could only send a quick loving glance towards the house with the green door where her cousin Jocelyn and his wife Felicity lived when they weren't working up in London, and another glance to the holy well with the pigeons circling round it, and then she was running down the High Street beside the little tinkling stream that came down from the hills, and that ran so fast along the gutter that even in this cold weather it was not frozen over.

But it was slow going, for even though the pavements had been swept they were very slippery and she was for ever skidding into

fat old gentlemen and sending them staggering into the heaps of snow beside the gutter; which annoyed them so much that she had to stop and apologize. "I'll never do it!" she gasped, cannonading off Mr. Wilkes, the landlord of the Green Dragon, the nicest hotel in Torminster. "Never! Oh, I beg your pardon, Mr. Wilkes. Oh, I *am* sorry! But I can't stop, I'm afraid. Good-bye."

But heaven was on her side and the train was late. Even though a further collision with the Archdeacon delayed her by a good five minutes (for you must stop to pick up an Archdeacon when you knock him over) she reached the platform just as it came steaming in; a very festive looking train with a glorious plume of blue smoke decorating the engine and a Christmas tree waving from one of the windows.

"That'll be Father!" thought Henrietta ecstatically, and sped down the platform.

Gabriel Ferranti left the train while it was still moving and stood with arms held wide, the Christmas tree brandished in one hand and a bag of oranges in the other. Henrietta, reaching him, leapt and clung, while his arms went round her, and the oranges and the Christmas tree fell unconsidered to the ground.

"Father!" panted Henrietta, subjecting him to a throttling embrace. "Father! How long are you staying?"

It was always her invariable, eager question, and it always cut her father to the heart … Because he had missed so many of the early years of her. Because he went away so much and, even now, often forgot about her. Because in all that he did and was he knew himself to be unstable as water … But this time, he vowed, he would spend an irreproachable Christmas holiday; bearing with Grandmother, going to church whenever Grandfather wished it, wiping his feet on the mat and being punctual for meals. And he would be utterly Henrietta's. All that she wanted him to do he would do, finishing it to the utmost with no untidy ends. He hugged her close, rejoicing in the delicious warmth of her, in the ecstatic beating of her heart under his hand and her soft cool cheek pressed tightly against his. "Have you good tidings, Angel Gabrielle?" he asked her.

Henrietta's other name was Gabrielle, after her father, but he was the only person whom she permitted to use it. That name of hers was his private property, she felt. It was a link between them. While he remembered his own name he would remember hers, and her.

"Good!" she said, hugging him. "You've come back … I've got a new coat. Do you like it?"

She wriggled away from him and pranced a few steps up the platform, holding the scarlet coat out wide.

"Grand," said Ferranti, "most Parisian … Why, the train's gone on with my luggage inside. 'Erb, why the dickens didn't you take my luggage out?"

"Didn't know you 'ad any, sir," said 'Erb, the beery, good-natured Torminster porter. "You mostly forgets to bring it when you comes. 'Sides, I'd me 'ands full with these 'ere oranges."

The bag had burst, Ferranti and Henrietta now perceived, and the whole personnel of the station, 'Erb, Mr. Heythrop the ticket collector, Mrs. Partridge from the waiting room and Tommy Higgins from the bookstall, were engaged in gathering them up before they rolled off on to the line. Ferranti's eccentric arrivals were always popular at the station for there was no knowing what he might bring with him as a present for the children; Hengist and Horsa the white mice, a puppy in a basket, a bowl of goldfish, a talking parrot; all these had arrived at various times and had given great pleasure at the station, though not to Grandmother later on.

"Never mind," said Henrietta maternally. "It'll come back by the next train. We'll send the oranges and the tree up in the bus, Father, so that Gotobed won't be disappointed at there being no luggage. Thank you, 'Erb. Thank you, Tommy. Will you bring them out to the bus?"

"Your ticket, sir," said Mr. Heythrop firmly.

"It's gone on," said Ferranti. "It was in the pocket of the overcoat that 'Erb didn't take out."

"Very good, sir," said Mr. Heythrop placidly. "I'll just make a note of that. Where's me pencil?"

"Have mine," said Henrietta helpfully. "It marks quite well if you suck it first."

"Thank you, miss, obliged I'm sure," said Mr. Heythrop and did as suggested.

Torminster was a quiet town, situated well off the beaten track. Life at the station was in consequence rather uneventful and any arrival was of great interest. The whole staff accompanied Ferranti and Henrietta out to the old pumpkin-shaped horse bus and helped them to explain to Mr. Gotobed, the portly worthy who drove it, about the luggage coming later, and the oranges and the tree to go now, and would he please say to Canon and Mrs. Fordyce that Mr. Ferranti and Miss Henrietta were walking up but would be careful not to be late for lunch.

"Right," said Mr. Gotobed, poising his top hat at an acute angle and taking a firm grip of his whip. "Oranges inside, 'Erb, tree up 'ere on the box. Looks festive like. All aboard? Right!" And he brought his whip down on the backs of the two fat bay horses and set the pumpkin-bus into such unusually rapid motion that it actually caught up with Ferranti and Henrietta by the time they reached the Market Place. But here, of course, it was obliged to slow down, for there was a slight slope from the Market Place to the Close, and the fat horses, their figures being what they were, knew the consideration due to them.

Henrietta and Ferranti crossed the Green towards the Cathedral, for Henrietta had explained about fetching the key. They walked slowly, hand in hand, telling each other about everything they had been doing since they last met, taking delighted stock of each other.

Henrietta saw with satisfaction that her father was just the same, tall and thin and untidy-looking, with the same crooked smile and twinkling eyes and jerky excited voice. Becoming famous had made no difference to him except that he looked stronger from having enough to eat, and his gay mad clothes, though still untidy, weren't quite as disreputable as they used to be. She was glad he did not change. That, she thought, was one of the satisfactory things about grown-ups; if they changed at all it was so slowly that one didn't notice it; while with little children you never knew where you were.

"Have I changed?" she asked anxiously.

"You're taller," said Ferranti, "and a little thinner, but that's all. You'll never change much, Angel Gabrielle. Your starriness is a quality of the mind, I think, not of the body. It'll only deepen as you grow older … Please God."

He spoke the last two words jerkily, as they passed through the west door and the great Cathedral gripped them. Quick to feel all that he felt she knew that he was afraid for her; afraid that life might treat her as badly as it had treated him in the old days.

"But they pass by, don't they," she said comfortingly.

"What pass by, Gabrielle?"

"The bad days."

"Yes, they pass by … Though to look at this place you wouldn't think so."

"The sun's gone in," said Henrietta, explaining the sudden oppression of the darkening Cathedral. "And there aren't many flowers about because it's Advent. It'll be darker still in the crypt."

"Aren't you scared to come here alone, you scrap?" asked Ferranti.

"No," said Henrietta. "At least I was a little scared this morning. Just for a minute. I don't know why."

It was, as Henrietta had expected, very dark in the crypt, but she had no difficulty in finding her way to the chapel because a line of light showed under the door.

"I can't have blown the candles out either!" exclaimed Henrietta. "Aren't I tiresome!"

"You're as absent-minded as your father," said Ferranti. "Shame on you!"

"But the door's a little bit open," said Henrietta, "and I *know* I shut the door!"

"Shocking," mocked Ferranti, but Henrietta was suddenly, once more, a little scared. She was glad her father was with her. She held on to him very tightly with one hand while she pushed open the door with the other.

And afterwards she was glad that she had, for had it not been for his grip on her she would certainly have cried out. For there was someone in the chapel; a man's figure crouched on the floor before the altar, in the same attitude, as though he had fallen forward while praying, in which they had found the dead body of Nicolas de Malden ... It *was* Nicolas de Malden ... No, it wasn't, it was the shabby grey-haired man who had wanted her to tell him about the dog in the chantry.

And then she suddenly found herself sitting half-way up the steps that led back to the nave, with her father beside her, and neither of them saying anything. The same instinct for flight had seized them at the same moment, and now the same instinct of pity had stayed them. And both of them were hot with shame. It is not often that one sees any one in a moment of misery, for they take good care one shall not, but if the sight is rare it is horribly unforgettable. They were so ashamed that they should have seen. Slowly they got up and climbed back to the nave.

"I saw him this morning," said Henrietta. "He was going round the Cathedral. I thought he looked hungry. Whatever shall we do? You must do something about it, Father! Do something about it!"

Ferranti pondered. Henrietta was very quickly wanting him to do something for her. Well, he must do it; and finish it with no untidy ends. "You go on home," he said, "and tell Grandmother I'm coming later. I'll stay here, and bump into him accidentally when he comes up. I might be able to pay for a meal as a start."

"Have you any money on you?" asked Henrietta.

"No. It was all in the coat that went on."

"Isn't that just like you!" said Henrietta with the irritability of extreme distress. "I've told you over and over again, Father, not to put things in your overcoat pockets … You're bound to lose the overcoat … But you never listen to a word I say!"

"Indeed I do, Angel," said her father humbly. "But I forget afterwards. Don't cry, Angel. Haven't *you* any money on you?"

"I must have the half-crown Grandmother gave me for the stamps somewhere," said Henrietta, and felt up her knickers (they had elastic at the knee and she kept lots of things up them), down her neck and in the pocket of her dress. "It was knotted into my handky," she sobbed, "and I'm wanting my handky!"

"Try your overcoat pocket," suggested Ferranti very gently.

Henrietta tried it, with success, and her lovely shining smile broke through her tears. "But I can't help it!" she chuckled. "I get it all from you!"

Ferranti chuckled too. He, like Henrietta, loved to discover links between them, even when the links were those of utter stupidity. "Run on home, Angel," he said. "And don't worry about that fellow down there. I'll see to him. And I won't forget to lock up the chapel and bring back the key."

Henrietta ran on home, quite happy again. She had confidence in her father. He might not be very good at catching trains, or keeping a firm hold of his possessions, but she had discovered already that when it came to dealing with humanity in distress he knew what to do. Both as a man and a writer he was experienced in distress.

"And where's your father?" asked Grandmother, meeting Henrietta at the front door. "Nothing's arrived but a lot of smashed oranges and a Christmas tree, and some confused message from Gotobed that I could make neither head nor tail of. Missed the train, I suppose?"

"No, Grandmother. Father was almost quite punctual. He would have been *quite* punctual if it hadn't been for the train being late."

"Then where's his luggage?"

"It's gone on."

"Gone on where?"

"To the next station. We forgot to take it out."

"Then where's your father now?"

"In the Cathedral."

"What's he doing?"

"Talking to a poor man who looked hungry."

Grandmother clicked her tongue in annoyance. "No consideration," she said. "It's of no use waiting lunch any longer. Ring the bell, Sarah. Run and wash, Henrietta. *Look* at your hands."

As Henrietta washed her hands she counted up to three hundred. This was a trick that Grandfather had taught her to keep down rising temper. She loved Grandmother very dearly, being well aware of the sterling goodness that existed under the little old lady's outward asperity. Grandmother was like a silver needle, bright and sharp but good metal right through, but when her little jabs were directed at Ferranti Henrietta had hard work to keep her temper. The amount of arithmetic she did when Ferranti was in the house was striking. Upon one occasion she had actually counted up to two thousand six hundred and fifty in one day; but that was the time when Ferranti had broken three china ornaments in three hours, and was quite phenomenal. "Three hundred and one, three hundred and two," she said, running down the stairs. "Three hundred and three, three hundred and four," and found herself in her place at table.

"For what we are about to receive," said Grandfather, "the Lord make us truly thankful."

Then they sat down and as it was steak and kidney pie Henrietta left off counting because steak and kidney pie always made her feel good-tempered.

"Where are my stamps, Henrietta?" asked Grandmother.

"I didn't get them, Grandmother. I gave the two and six to Father to get some food for the hungry-looking man."

"Had your father no money of his own?"

"Yes, Grandmother, of course, but it went on."

"Went on where?"

"To the next station. I told you, Grandmother, that we forgot to take his luggage out."

Grandfather, perceiving that Grandmother's eyes were snapping and that Henrietta, laying down her knife and fork, had begun to count again, hastily intervened.

"Very considerate of the dear boy to deal with the poor fellow personally," said Grandfather. "Had he brought him home to lunch I doubt if the steak and kidney would have held out ... Not with Hugh Anthony's appetite what it is."

"Brought him home to lunch!" cried Grandmother in horror. "Some dreadful tramp! I never heard of such a thing!"

"But the dear boy has spared you the inconvenience, dear," said Grandfather.

There was a distinct softening in Grandmother. "Sarah," she said, "keep what's left of the steak and kidney hot for Mr. Ferranti."

"About this poor man, dear," said Grandfather to Henrietta. "What sort of a poor man?"

Henrietta just repeated that he was a poor man; she said nothing about the chapel. It was her habit to tell Grandfather everything, but this time she thought she wouldn't, for she thought it would be nice for Father to help the man by himself, without any interference from Grandfather. For Grandfather delighted to help people in distress; he was, in fact, downright greedy about it; and had he been told of the trouble the poor man was undoubtedly in he would have been off to the Cathedral like a hound on the scent of a fox. And then Father would have had to play second fiddle, and she wasn't going to have him play second fiddle. She smiled very sweetly at Grandfather and then filled her mouth so very full of baked apple that it was quite impossible for him to ask her any more questions.

Ferranti, looking extraordinarily pleased with himself, arrived just as they were finishing up their water biscuits and Cheddar cheese. He greeted Grandmother with great deference, smiled at Henrietta, pulled Hugh Anthony's hair, and turned to wring the hand of Grandfather, whom he loved best in the world after Henrietta and the poet's craft. Grandfather beamed behind his spectacles. Ferranti was as a son to him and he knew of no greater joy on earth than the return of prosperous and happy children to the home that he kept always in readiness for their welcome and refreshment.

Grandfather and the children sat with Ferranti while he ate his hotted-up pie, but Grandmother, who took no pleasure in watching poets feed, went off to her after-dinner forty-winks.

"Could you lend me twenty pounds, Grandfather?" Ferranti, owing to Grandmother's absence, was able to ask.

"Certainly, dear boy," said Grandfather instantly, but his eyes popped slightly behind their glasses.

"And is there a step-ladder in the house that I could borrow later on?" continued Ferranti.

"Certainly, dear boy," said Grandfather, and his eyes popped even more.

"I shall be running up to London by the afternoon train," said Ferranti airily. "It's all right, Angel, it's only to fetch some things I shall be needing. Paints, and that. I'll be back to-morrow."

"Paints?" queried Grandfather. "I didn't know you painted."

"I daub a bit now and then," said Ferranti. "Mustard, please, Hugh Anthony."

"But you could have my paint-box," said Henrietta.

"Mine, too," said Hugh Anthony magnanimously … He hated painting.

"They wouldn't be quite adequate," said Ferranti.

"Why?"

"Because they wouldn't."

"Why?"

"Could I have some more of that pie?" asked Ferranti.

"And about that poor fellow, the tramp," said Grandfather, returning to the subject next his heart at the moment. "Have you done everything possible for him? Could I be of any assistance?"

"He's all right," said Ferranti. "No need to worry about him. Could you fetch me a drawing-board, kids, and a large sheet of drawing paper? I must catch the three o'clock train and I have something to do in the town first."

"But surely you're not taking the board and paper up to London?" queried Grandfather, more bewildered than ever.

"I'll drop them on the way," said Ferranti. "And a pencil, Angel. The one you lent to Mr. Heythrop will do."

In ten minutes' time he was gone, carrying the drawing paper and board, the pencil and the twenty pounds, and wearing Grandfather's second-best overcoat because it was beginning to snow again. Grandfather watched him go with some anxiety, for really Ferranti's tall thin figure, burdened with the drawing-board and buttoned into an overcoat several sizes too small, looked remarkably odd. Almost he inclined to Grandmother's consistently held opinion that all geniuses, especially poets, are stark, staring mad.

Henrietta was more than anxious, she was unhappy, for she was dreadfully afraid that Father might forget to come back in the morning; and he was also, she was quite sure, keeping something from her, and it made her feel positively ill to have things kept from her. Also she couldn't find her precious drawing, her design for the east wall of the chapel; she must have left it in the chapel but she couldn't go and retrieve it because Father had gone off with the key. Life, she thought, was hard. She cried, secretly of course, when she went to bed; nothing gave her any comfort; not even the fact that it was now so cold that Grandmother said that just to-night she need not wash at all.

Chapter V

But things were better next day. In the morning Ferranti's luggage came back; and such is the honesty of the west country that his money was still intact in his overcoat pocket; in the afternoon she and Hugh Anthony planted the Christmas tree in a pot, and felt very nice and festive, and at seven o'clock in the evening Ferranti came back minus the twenty pounds and minus also, as far as one could see, anything in the way of paints to show for it. Asked what he had done with them he seemed not to know; asked what he had been doing with himself between the hour of five, when the London train reached Torminster, and seven, when he turned up at the house, he seemed not to know either. Grandmother's worst suspicions as to his mental derangement were completely confirmed and Henrietta was more than ever certain that he was keeping something from her … When he came up to her bedroom to say good-night after dinner that night he found her sitting up in bed, shivering with the cold, her pink flannel dressing-gown draped round her shoulders and her eyes suspiciously bright. She must, however, have been lying down earlier, because there was a wet patch on her pillow.

"Have you been crying, Angel?" he asked.

"No," said Henrietta firmly.

"Of course not," said Ferranti. "I am sorry to have voiced so unworthy a suspicion."

"I never cry," said Henrietta with increasing firmness. "Not at my age."

"Of course not," repeated Ferranti. "Please forgive me for that merely momentary doubt."

"It was because you have a secret and you haven't told it to me," said Henrietta, blinking her eyelashes.

"What was?"

"That I—that I—"

"That you didn't cry?"

"Yes."

"Some of it is to do with Christmas, Gabrielle. You shall know at Christmas. But some of it you shall know now. And, what's more, you'll have to help me with it."

"Oh!" cried Henrietta, and bounced in bed.

"I thought you'd like that," said Ferranti, and then, "Are no fires allowed in Torminster bedrooms? Is warmth definitely un-Christian?"

"Visitors have the oil stove in the spare room if they are delicate," said Henrietta, twinkling. "Do you feel delicate, Father?"

"I feel extremely debilitated," said Ferranti. "Stay there, Angel. I'll tap on the wall when I'm ready, and then we'll have a party."

Chuckling, Henrietta cuddled down in bed and listened through the crack of the door to Ferranti outside on the landing, calling over the banisters to Sarah and coughing very painfully. "I've a cold coming on, Sarah. Could I have the oil stove in the spare room?"

"Ah," said Sarah portentously from below, "It's bronchial."

"The oil stove?"

"No, sir, your chest," said Sarah. "It's only what's to be expected with you leaving your overcoat in the train the way you did ... Better have a mustard plaster on it," she added, warming to the subject, for affliction of any sort was always a pleasure to her. "There was my sister's youngest was dead in a week. Bronchial, and worked inward as you might say. I'll be up in a minute, sir, with the stove and the mustard."

Ferranti stopped coughing and sneezed. "It's in my head," he averred. "There's no need for a mustard plaster, Sarah, but what about a whisky and soda?"

"No intoxicating liquors are ever served in *this* 'ouse, sir," said Sarah severely, "and that you know well. Not unless it's serious illness; and if you'll excuse me saying so, sir, I doubt if you're that far gone as yet. But an 'ot lemon drink the mistress permits, sir, if desired, and I'll be up with it in a minute, together with an 'ot bottle and the stove. I shouldn't 'ang about on the landing, sir, if I was you. Early to bed is what's best with these 'ead colds."

"No, Sarah, thank you, Sarah," said Ferranti, and went into his room blowing his nose.

Henrietta listened with delight to the sounds of preparation for the party; Sarah coming up with the stove, and matches being struck to the accompaniment of volleys of sneezes from Ferranti; Sarah going down again and coming up afresh; then more sneezes and the clink of a silver spoon against a glass; then Sarah's final departure and Ferranti tapping on the wall.

She wrapped her eiderdown about her and scurried in. The spare room, ancient and austere, with dark beams crossing a whitewashed ceiling and an old oak floor that waved up and down like the waves of the sea, looked lovely lit by the glow of the stove and by the candles in silver candlesticks that burned on the old-fashioned dressing-table and chest-of-drawers. And Ferranti, dressed in the evening dress that Grandmother, a great champion of social correctitude, always insisted upon for dinner, looked curiously suited by the room. But then, she reflected, he always did look suited by his environment. It was because he liked it and made use of it, whatever it might be, absorbed it into himself and used it as his artist's material. She was like that, too. Wherever she went she looked, marvelled and adored, and then stored away in her memory the essential beauty of what she had seen, so that one day she might take it out and make it into pictures ... As now she was storing away in her memory the reflections of the candle flames on the dark polished floor, the rosy glow of the stove on the whitewashed ceiling, and her father's face lit by the light that only came upon it when they were going to have one of their glorious secret times.

It was only he who gave her these particular glorious times. She had glorious times with Grandfather, and with Hugh Anthony, but they weren't quite the same, not so exciting. Such things as midnight feasts, or walks by moonlight, had a little lost their attraction for Grandfather now that he was eighty, and adventures with Hugh Anthony were sometimes marred by violent disagreement as to what it would be nice to do next. But Ferranti, who now that success and happiness had come into his life seemed sometimes like a man born again, was still full of youthful eagerness and yet at the same time quite willing to have it guided by Henrietta.

They sat down on the sofa and Henrietta drank the hot lemon drink, absorbing it slowly and blissfully, savouring each sip. She adored hot lemon but didn't get it unless she had a cold, or unless Hugh Anthony had a cold and gave her his. Her father watched her absorbed, eager little face, her deep concentration on her pleasure. Everything she did she was able to do with her whole soul. The world, he thought, would be the gladder for her coming into it.

"There!" she said, putting the glass down with a long, satisfied sigh. "Now tell me the secret. Tell it like a story."

Ferranti was a most accomplished story-teller, above all by candlelight, a light which is romantic above all others; a gentle light into which fairies and ghosts are not afraid to step at the summons of the story-teller. Bright daylight hurts their eyes, unattuned to the glare of this world, and is inclined too to dazzle the eyes of mortal folk so that they can see only the hardest of outlines, chairs and tables and trees, and not the tenuous frail outline of something that has no physical substance ... Candlelight is the best for tales ... Henrietta wriggled closer to her father, within the shelter of his arm lest there should be ghosts in the story, and looked with delicious tingling anticipation at the shadows that might presently take shape and form and be one knew not who.

"We'll have to begin with a dull story," said Ferranti, "the true one that you asked for and that is part of the secret that I was keeping from you. We'll get on to ghosts and so on later."

"But true stories are often just as wonderful as fairy ones," said Henrietta. "The Christmas story, with the angels and shepherds, that's true, and yet it's really just as exciting as fairies. Go on, Father, begin."

"This one," persisted Ferranti, "is dull; though I'm hoping that there'll be an ending yet to come that will be rather exciting … There was once a man whose greatest joy in life was painting pictures."

"Oh!" thrilled Henrietta. Her greatest joy in life was painting pictures, so already she loved this man.

"Don't interrupt," said Ferranti. "If you interrupt I shall spank you … Well, in some ways this man was rather unfortunate because no one wanted to buy the pictures that he painted, and as he had to support himself and his family this was rather awkward, because if people don't give you money for the work you do you starve, and so does your family, and you don't like that and nor do they. All artists, whether they are musicians or painters or writers, experience the same difficulty. I did when nobody would buy my poems, and I expect you will too when you grow up and paint your pictures. It's a difficulty that passes, of course, for one of three things is bound to happen fairly soon; either the artist, under pressure of starvation, gives up painting the pictures he wants to paint, but can't sell, and paints those that he does not want to paint but can sell; or else he manages to last out until the public, having got accustomed to the kind of art that they formerly reviled, suddenly change their minds and like it after all; or else, remaining true to the kind of work he likes and not having the kind of body that will last out unfed while the public slowly change their mind, he dies."

"But there's another thing he could do," said Henrietta eagerly, "he could give up being an artist and do something quite different; he could be a ticket-collector or a pork butcher."

"No," said Ferranti sombrely, "with an artist that is only another form of death. I've tried it and I know."

Henrietta wriggled closer. "It's all right now, Father," she whispered. "You lasted out and they liked you in the end."

"Yes," said Ferranti, "but we are not talking about me but about this man."

"What did he do?" asked Henrietta.

"Well, if he'd only had himself to think about he'd have chosen the second way, and if that had failed he would willingly have accepted the third, but you see he hadn't only himself to think about, he had a family, and so he chose the first way."

"He made pictures that he didn't want to make?"

"Yes."

Ferranti seemed to have a certain difficulty in getting to the next stage of the story and Henrietta had to prompt him.

"Well," she said, "what happened then?"

"It's difficult to explain," said Ferranti. "Do you know what integrity is?"

"Is it telling the truth?" asked Henrietta. "Grandfather told me once but I forget."

"It means a lot more than that. A man's integrity means his constancy in service to his own vision of what is true. And every man has a rather different vision, Gabrielle, and serves it in a rather different way. Grandfather, for instance, has his vision and serves it in his way, the way of the priest. I have mine, quite different from his, and serve it as a poet. We both of us have a certain skill and use it to the utmost to express what we have seen; that is our integrity; but if for the sake of greed or ambition we were to use that skill to express a vision that was not our own, or to express a perversion of our vision, then our integrity would be lost."

"And the man lost his?" asked Henrietta pitifully.

"Yes. He deliberately chose to lose it."

"But he did it to help his family!" cried Henrietta with warm championship.

"That is what is called an extenuating circumstance," said Ferranti, "but it didn't make any difference to the fact that he lost it; and when you lose your integrity, Angel, you get less and less of a man and find it harder and harder to distinguish between good and evil. This man finally found it so hard that he just came to grief altogether."

"How?" asked Henrietta.

"He broke the law and was punished for it, and now the poor chap is worse off than ever he was."

"But if he's been punished, now he can begin again," said Henrietta. "He can start painting the right kind of pictures and get back his what's-its-name."

"Integrity."

"Yes."

"That's what he feels, too, but how can he when he hasn't got the money to buy paints and things? You've no idea, Angel, how difficult it is to have anything at all, even integrity, if you haven't got any money."

"It's perfectly easy," said Henrietta. "Give him the money."

"I tried that, but he won't take it. He's one of those proud blokes who won't be helped."

Henrietta gave an impatient exclamation, but was not nonplussed. "Give him a what-do-you-call-it—a commission. Ask him to paint a picture for you, the right kind of picture, and pay him for it. If you haven't got the money just at the moment, you can borrow enough to go on with from Grandfather."

"Hurrah!" cried Ferranti. "That's just what I have done!"

"I knew it! I knew it!" cried Henrietta, leaping from the eiderdown to subject her parent to a strangling embrace. "And the man is the man in the chapel! Say he's the man in the chapel! Isn't he?"

"Got it in one," said Ferranti.

"Oh! Oh!" cried Henrietta. "And you borrowed my drawing paper and board for him to make a start, and then you went up to London to buy the paints. I see! I see! And what picture will he paint, Father? What picture will he paint?"

"A portrait of my daughter, a Christmas present for Grandfather," said Ferranti. "He and I are both agreed that it shall be a portrait of my daughter."

Henrietta was a little crestfallen. "That won't do," she said. "That won't do at all. A portrait of me won't be a picture of a vision, and you said that to have integrity a man must paint a vision."

"How do you know you're not a vision?" asked her infatuated parent.

"But I'm not, I'm just me."

"Artists often see visions when they see a certain face. It seems that this man did, when he saw yours in the Cathedral."

"What did he see?"

"The description he gave was rather confused. But it had wings in it, and you of course, and a dog. I couldn't make it out."

"I hope the dog was Eric?"

"He didn't mention any particular name."

"But is he going to paint the vision, or only me?"

"He's starting on you."

"When?"

"To-morrow."

"Where?"

"In a studio I've hired for him here in Torminster. I'll take you to sit for him."

"Oh!" cried Henrietta, jumping up and down. "Was there ever anything so exciting? Are we to tell Grandfather?"

"Not just yet," said Ferranti. "It's to be a secret to surprise him at Christmas."

"And now you've told me all the story except the part that I'm not to know till Christmas. What is that?"

"How can I tell you now when you're not to know till Christmas?"

"Oh," groaned Henrietta. "Four weeks, four whole weeks to wait!"

"Curl up again," commanded Ferranti, "and I'll tell you a ghost story to quiet you down."

He told her a very thrilling ghost story, a story which made the shadows in the corners of the room take instant life and form, but she couldn't manage to be as deliciously terrified by them as she would have liked because her mind was so full of the other story, the true one. It was so wonderful to think that her father was giving the artist back his what's-its-name, and wonderful to think she was going to have her portrait painted. She was not a vain child, and she did not gloat over this latter fact because she wanted to know just exactly how pretty she was; she gloated over it because now, for the first time in her life, she was to go to a real studio and see a real painter at work. A studio, she knew, would be her own future kingdom. To-morrow she would catch a glimpse of this kingdom, see a sort of shadow play of her own future life.

"Now you must go to bed," said Ferranti, picking her up.

"So must you," said Henrietta. "Or stay in your room."

"But it's only half-past nine. The Cathedral's just struck."

"But you can't go back to the drawing-room again after making all that fuss about your cold on the landing. Sarah will have told Grandfather and Grandmother about your cold. They'll be very interested."

"How hard up you are for interest in Cathedral towns."

Henrietta looked up at him in surprise as he carried her to her room. Of course it was interesting when somebody had a cold, even if it were only a cold he'd invented. They had the sense to be very interested in everything in Torminster. The opening of a new flower thrilled them, and the rising of the moon. A cold in the head was a matter of much importance, and a birth or a death shook the whole community to its foundations. This, Henrietta thought, was as it should be.

Ferranti tucked her up in bed with his own hot-water bottle, she only being allowed bed-socks by the rule of the house, and bent down to kiss her. "I suppose," he said irrelevantly, "that Grandfather won't ask for the key of the chapel back?"

"He never remembers to ask for anything back," said Henrietta. "But you must give it him back, Father."

"In due course," said Ferranti, and kissed her again. She could feel the tingling warmth of his happiness.

"You liked telling that man to paint a picture of me," she stated.

"Yes, Gabrielle. You see I was once in a mess myself, and Grandfather and other people helped me out. I can't repay my debt to the people to whom I really owe it, one seldom can in this world, but I can in a sense repay it to somebody else. Do you see what I mean?"

Henrietta quite saw. But she also saw that he could have paid a little of his debt to Grandfather by being less evasive about her school bills, and more punctual at meals. She didn't say so, of course. She had accepted him as he was with all his failings as well as his nobilities, and loved him for the first almost as much as for the second. "You're nice," she told him. "You're very nice, and so is your hot-water bottle. Good-night, darling Father"

"Good-night, darling daughter. Do I pull your curtains back?"

"Yes, I like to see the stars. What shall I wear to be painted in? My new frock with the pink frills?"

"Good gracious no! I loathe those pink frills. Wear your starriest expression, and your red jersey."

"But it's so old!"

"When you're a painter, Gabrielle, you'll soon discover that old clothes are the best. Colours need to have the hardness taken out of them by sun and rain before they are really beautiful."

"I'll wear what you like," said Henrietta, "but I like pink frills."

He blew out the candle, pulled back the curtains, laughed and left her, and she heard him moving about in his room, and then the creak of the old arm-chair as he settled into it. Perhaps he was reading, she thought, or perhaps he was writing. On second thoughts she was sure he was writing; making a sonnet or a lyric, or a play in verse, or a novel that in a year's time the whole world would be reading. When she had been younger, quite a little girl, she had sometimes seen a ghost in that room, a grey monk who sat painting gay flowers and birds and beasts in the margin of a big book. She had never been frightened of him, for always he had been absorbed and happy, and seemingly quite unaware of her presence. When she had told Grandfather about him, Grandfather had said that he wasn't a real man at all, but just a sort of photograph of the past, a photograph of a real man who had once sat in his cell, built where their spare room was now, painting as she saw him paint. One did sometimes see these photographs, especially when one was a little child. Grandfather had not known who the man was, but now she suddenly wondered if he was Nicolas de Malden in his happy days, those days before he became a leper and went to live in the crypt. She shivered, thinking of him as a leper, slowly dying down there in the darkness. Yet, perhaps, he hadn't been so unhappy after all, because all the time he had been making something beautiful. Thinking of those angels and demons in the chapel she was quite sure that he had painted his vision exactly as he had seen it. He had kept his (what did her father call it?) integrity until he died.

Life might be terrible sometimes, as terrible as she had felt it to be when she went into the Cathedral yesterday morning, but it was nice to think how people could comfort themselves by making things. Lying revelling in the luxury of Ferranti's hot-water bottle she pictured him sitting perhaps exactly where Nicolas de Malden had sat, making a book, just as Nicolas had done. And then she pictured the unknown artist sitting in the studio that Ferranti had found for him, busy perhaps with the paper and pencil she had sent him, thinking just how he would pose a little girl next morning. And then she thought of Grandmother and Grandfather one on each side of the drawing-room fire. Grandmother would be knitting, and counting out loud, and enjoying it, and Grandfather would be fast asleep, his mouth wide open and his hands clasped upon his stomach; but even in his sleep he would be creating, polishing up tarnished souls, mending broken lives, planting bulbs and writing next Sunday's sermon. And Hugh Anthony? He would be in bed, his red head startlingly bright on the pillow, Hengist and Horsa beside him and his clothes strewn all over the floor. But he was probably awake, and mentally practising his bowling.

And last of all she thought of the second Nicolas of whose tragedy she knew just a little and no more. Was he making anything? She didn't know. He was lost, perhaps he was dead. She moved restlessly and saw the stars twinkling between the drawn curtains.

And the moon was shining too. She pictured Torminster lying under the moonlight, its steep roofs white and sparkling with frosted snow, its lighted windows patches of orange upon the shadowed walls, the great Cathedral cutting patterns out of the sky with its towers and pinnacles and the tall houses throwing blue shadows across the snowy streets. Torminster was making itself very beautiful to greet the rising moon, creating ever shifting patterns of loveliness, quite uncaring that there was no one but the moon to see … It was creating, and that was enough for Torminster.

Ten o'clock struck from the Cathedral, ten booming strokes that fell through the night as though ten great stars dropped from the sky, and a moment later Henrietta heard the drawing-room door shut and Grandmother's and Grandfather's feet on the stairs. Life at Torminster was entirely ruled by the Cathedral clock and they were never later than ten o'clock in going to bed. Henrietta could hear Grandfather's voice murmuring and knew that he was saying Compline. "I will lay me down in peace and take my rest, for it is Thou, Lord, only, that makest me dwell in safety."

Henrietta turned over and fell asleep.

Chapter VI

It was not a nice day next morning. It was beginning to thaw and the world that for the last week, with the sunshine and the frost, had been sparkling bright and full of wonder, looked drab and dirty. Even the garden looked dirty, with patches of brown earth showing through the white like spots of mud on a clean pinafore. The bright sky was hidden by dark lowering clouds that seemed unable to make up their minds whether they should send rain or sleet down to the earth, but were quite decided that whatever they sent it should be something unpleasant.

Henrietta was generally depressed by these drab days when the beauty of the earth seemed suddenly to go out like a blown candle-flame, but to-day, this day when she was to enter a painter's kingdom for the first time, she couldn't possibly feel depressed. On the contrary, as she put on the abbreviated dark-blue skirt and the old red jersey that her father liked, she was singing like a blackbird. But everyone else, except Hugh Anthony, seemed a little depressed at breakfast; even Ferranti, who had managed to be almost punctual and was very low in his mind in consequence.

Punctuality, he had once told Henrietta, always depressed him for it accentuated the passage of time, and the passing of time, to a man like Ferranti, is depressing. If, for instance, Ferranti had argued, you were punctual for lunch then you had compressed your morning into a bare three or four hours—it was gone in no time, but if you were very late for lunch your morning became correspondingly elastic, and so on through the day. But what of the night? Henrietta had asked. At that rate one would have to steal from the night, for one wouldn't get supper till close on midnight. And why not? Ferranti had answered. By all means let us cheat the night, for what is the night but a thief who steals from us some of the few precious hours lent us for work and love. Henrietta, who was attached to her sleep, both because it made her feel refreshed and strong, and because in it she visited wonderful places, saw lovely sights and heard wonderful sounds, had opened her mouth to argue further, but had desisted … It is never much use arguing with poets.

But since punctuality depresses them one has to exert oneself at breakfast time to cheer them up, and Henrietta exerted herself. She was also particularly loving to Grandfather and Grandmother, who were feeling the change in the weather in their sciatic nerves. Though she was not naturally high-spirited she was one of those lucky people who can express love at will; it did not muzzle her as it does some unfortunates, it took the nature deliberately yielded to it and played upon it as an expert violinist upon his instrument.

Hugh Anthony, though he was, as always, feeling pleased with life, made no conscious effort to communicate his pleasure. This he left to Henrietta, for he was not, as she was, distressed by other people's low spirits. If they failed to be excited by this exciting world that, he thought, was their fault, and he saw no reason why he should put himself out to make them share in his own happy sensations. Yet there were few who were not persuaded to happiness by Hugh Anthony. The flaming hair, the freckled eager face, the bright blue eyes, the incessantly enquiring mind; these things could not fail to refresh. They warmed as a fire warms, burning unconsciously, comforting only those who seek it out, while Henrietta's radiance was as a lamp that is deliberately lit and carried to the place where the shadows are darkest.

"Why can't I go with you to wherever it is you are going?" Hugh Anthony asked Henrietta. He was not aggrieved, nor jealous, for aggrievement and jealousy were foreign to his nature; he was merely wanting to know.

"Because it has to do with Christmas, and you can't keep a secret," said Henrietta.

Hugh Anthony sighed, and reached for the honey. It was quite true that he couldn't keep a secret. Just as he couldn't bear any one to know anything he didn't know so he couldn't bear to know anything that they didn't know. The acquiring and imparting of information was a passion with him.

"Never mind, Hugh Anthony," said Grandfather, "you and I will have a Christmas secret together to surprise Henrietta. And it won't matter if you let it out."

Henrietta reached for Grandfather's hand under the table and squeezed it in a passion of gratitude. When her father came she always felt a little apologetic towards Grandfather, Grandmother and Hugh Anthony, the three who loved her and were with her always, because she had to neglect them for her father. But Grandfather always understood. He made it easy for her to do private things with Ferranti, he soothed Grandmother's irritation at Ferranti's habits and saw to it that Hugh Anthony did not miss her companionship. He stepped aside from her life when her father was with her, but when Ferranti had gone, promising to write and then forgetting to, he stepped back, and seemed to grow to a greater stature, filling his own place in her life and Ferranti's vacated niche as well, so that she could not feel lonely or forsaken … A great man, Grandfather.

"If wherever you're going is out of doors," said Grandmother severely to Ferranti, "you and Henrietta must wrap up well, for a thaw is to my mind more conducive to a chill than is a frost, and Sarah tells me you had a severe cold last night, though I must say I see few signs of it this morning … And please to remember that lunch is at one."

Ferranti bowed, Henrietta bolted the last mouthful of bread and marmalade, and they were allowed at Henrietta's request to "get down." They almost ran through the garden, such an eagerness possessed them, through the Close and across the Cathedral Green.

"Where is the studio?" gasped Henrietta.

"In the Market Place. Mary and Martha have taken him as a lodger. The studio is over the sweet-shop."

"Good," said Henrietta. "I shall be able to watch the pigeons flying round the holy well and play with the sweet-shop kittens, and Martha will bring me up sweets to eat."

They ran under the archway that led from the Green to the Market Place and pushed open the sweet-shop door, Henrietta pausing to jump up and down on the door mat, it being one of those exciting door mats which ring a bell when jumped upon.

Martha and Mary had kept the sweet-shop for years and years. Mary, who was between ninety and a hundred, did not now emerge from the back room, where she sat severely enthroned in her arm-chair surrounded by a family of kittens which seemed to visitors to be the same family in a state of miraculously preserved youth but were in fact a never-ending succession of different families, all the progeny of the same excellent and persevering mother, Cornelia, the sweet-shop cat, whose devotion to duty even though she was not now so young as she once had been, was an example to all. So was Martha's. Even though she was now very old, a white-haired old lady made, apparently, of Dresden china, her zeal in the matter of selling sweets to little children was as unflagging as her zeal in retailing gossip. She was an incomparable gossip. She could add two and three together and make six better than any one else in Torminster, and yet the addition was entirely without malice; reputations and characters, in Martha's hands, were merely enhanced in glory and virtue.

Yet she could, if bound to secrecy, keep the promise she had made. It was agony to her but she could do it. She had character. The moment Ferranti and Henrietta came into the shop Martha popped up from behind the jars of coloured sweets on the counter like a jack-in-the-box. She was evidently most excited for her lace cap was askew and her spectacles pushed up on her forehead; and her knitting, Henrietta saw, was in a state of great confusion owing, no doubt, to the position of the spectacles.

She put her finger on her lip, looked all round to see that no intruder had entered, shooed out a ginger kitten who had, and spoke. "He had two eggs to his breakfast," she whispered. "Not a soul's seen him."

"That's good," said Ferranti. "Shall we go up now? What'll you have to eat, Gabrielle, while you're sitting? You'll get hungry."

"One ounce of satin prauleens," said Henrietta, who always knew her own mind. Satin prauleens were delicious squares of coloured sugar, hard outside and soft inside. Nowhere throughout the length and breadth of England could one find such satin prauleens as were found at the sweet-shop. For size, colour and flavour they were incomparable.

Henrietta received her sustenance in a pink paper bag and followed Ferranti up the long flight of twisty stairs to the big attic at the top of the house. Her heart was beating very fast. When the door opened she would see not what she had last seen, an empty room, filled with old sweet tins, but the kingdom to which she belonged.

Yet when Ferranti had knocked and they had gone in she was suddenly so alarmed that she could not look. She stood behind her father with her eyes downcast, clutching her bag of sweets. She was frightened for several reasons; partly she was scared of the man whom she had last seen in such grief in the chapel, scared of his grief, greatly ashamed of having seen it; and partly, now that she was about to enter into her kingdom, she was afraid of it, subconsciously aware of the demands it would make upon her life, and the disappointment and labour she would have to endure before she could make it her own. She hesitated to enter into it … Very suddenly and unexpectedly she wanted Grandmother.

"What is the matter, Angel?" asked Ferranti. "Come on!" And he firmly pulled her in front of him, his hands reassuringly on her shoulders.

"You're not frightened of me, are you?" asked another voice. "I'd hoped you would tell me about Eric."

Eric did the trick. Henrietta suddenly felt at home and looked up gratefully at the man in front of her. He was smiling and looked now very far from grief-stricken, indeed quite the contrary. The two eggs to his breakfast must have done it. She returned his smile and looked cautiously beyond him at the room. Not much to be seen yet; only brushes, palettes and tubes of paint, a sheet of paper pinned to her own drawing-board, with already the outline of a child's head and shoulders sketched upon it, and a great stretched, untouched sheet of paper fastened to a huge board upon an easel. But Henrietta was thrilled. These were the artist's tools. With them he told of his visions and fought his battles with his own ignorance and blindness. They were his words and his weapons. One day they would be hers. She went from one to the other of them, touching them. When she got to the big empty sheet of paper she stopped, staring at it, filling it with form and colour, her eyes at first dreaming, then quick and alive as they followed her vision over the canvas. The two men watched her entranced.

"Why!" she cried suddenly, pointing to a piece of paper that was fastened with a drawing pin to the easel. "It's mine! It's my drawing that I lost! My picture for the chapel wall!"

The strange man was beside her with two strides.

"*You* drew that?" he demanded. "A scrap like you?"

Henrietta was indignant. She was not a scrap. She was eleven and tall for her age. "Of course," she said with dignity. "Why shouldn't I draw it?" Then anguish suddenly seized her. "It's bad!" she cried. Pinned there beside that empty, hungry sheet of paper she saw its childishness and futility in all their horror. *That* to portray the vision she had seen in her mind! *That* to tell of what might have been painted upon the east wall! "It doesn't say it!" she cried. "It doesn't say it!" and burst into tears.

Her father picked her up, sat her in the window seat, and administered a black kitten with a white patch over its eye, mercifully present at the time, but the artist tactfully took no notice of her. He went on staring at the crude little drawing and at the empty sheet of paper, brooding over them.

"Where does she get it from, Ferranti?" he asked.

"Get what from?"

"Her genius."

125

"From me, of course," said Ferranti with a certain smugness. "I've had her taught," he added with a good deal of self-satisfaction ... But that, as it happened, was not strictly true; he had suggested that Henrietta should have drawing lessons, but after that he had suffered from his habitual loss of memory and it was Grandfather who had had to pay for them.

"But you don't paint, do you?" asked the artist.

"I write," said Ferranti firmly. "It's the same thing, coming out a bit different in the next generation."

"Indeed?" said the artist politely; so very politely that it seemed he disagreed with Ferranti.

Henrietta paid no attention to what they were saying. She was very ashamed of having cried, and very busy trying to conquer the subsequent hiccups. "I beg your pardon," she said to her host when she had subdued them.

"Not at all," he said. "Personally, when I feel as you did, I knock things down. Crying is really less destructive." He turned to Ferranti. "I'll get started on the portrait," he said. "There's no need to keep you," he added kindly but firmly.

Ferranti arose in some dudgeon, experiencing to the full those emotions felt by a lover when another man endeavours to supplant him in the affections of the beloved. "I shall be back in an hour to rescue her," he said with equal firmness. "She'll get tired if she sits too long."

"She won't," said the man. "She's an artist."

When Ferranti had gone a quiet absorbed peace fell upon the room. Two enthusiasts were together, with no disturbing element. Henrietta took off her coat and cap and sat perfectly still and quiet on the chair put for her, the kitten asleep on her lap and her sweets beside her for refreshment later on.

The painter, as he mixed his water colours and began his portrait, had upon his face that set, almost locked look that she had seen upon her father's face when he was writing, upon Grandfather's when he prayed and Hugh Anthony's when he studied cricket scores. She expected that she had it when she was drawing. She always thought she felt a sort of click in her head when she concentrated her attention upon this work that of all others meant most to her; as though her mind and her work locked together and a key had actually turned ... It was a good feeling.

But presently, she saw, the painter's face looked less set. She knew what he was feeling now. The first difficult push-off was over and his mind and his body were working in perfect adjustment, like two wings that carried his invention smoothly and well. She dared to speak.

"Oughtn't I to call you something?" she inquired. "I don't think it is very respectful of me not to call you anything."

"You might call me John," said the painter. "That happens to be my name."

"But I can't call you that," protested Henrietta. "That would not be respectful either when you are so old. I shall call you Fra Angelico. He was a great painter, you know. They called him the Brother of the Angels because he painted angels so beautifully ... I'm sure you paint angels beautifully."

The painter suddenly stopped working and looked at her. It was a flinching sort of look, almost as though she had pleased him so much that it hurt. "Nice little kid," he muttered. "Painted angels well, did he? I'll paint you damn' well or perish in the attempt ... Keep still now ... And don't talk about respecting me for my great age. Artists respect one another for their work, don't they, not for their age or their wealth or anything like that. I respect you for that drawing that I picked up on the chapel floor; but whether you will ever respect me I don't know. We'll have to see when I've finished the portrait."

Henrietta was pleased. Here was one of those sensible grown-ups who was going to treat her as an equal, just as Grandfather and Ferranti did, and not talk down to her as though not having lived so very long in this world made her somehow an inferior being to himself. Henrietta never could see that being grown-up was anything to boast about. One didn't grow oneself, adding to one's inches by one's own skill. God grew one.

"You're a water colour artist?" Fra Angelico asked her very seriously.

"Yes," answered Henrietta. "Like yourself."

"It's my favourite medium," he said. "You've not tried oils yet?"

"I don't mean to," said Henrietta firmly. "Too sticky."

"A little thick, perhaps," said Fra Angelico. "One can achieve brightness and purity of colour more easily with water colour I think."

"Why did you start on my portrait before I'd even got here?" asked Henrietta.

"I began the very night after I'd just seen you. I couldn't wait."

"But why?"

Fra Angelico actually paused in his work to answer. "I'll tell you. When you saw me in the Cathedral I was planning a picture in my head, a Christmas picture, the adoration at the manger, but I could not get the vision of it clear in my mind ... Once it had been clear but I had lost it ... And when I saw you it was suddenly clear again; the whole thing fell into place, so to speak, with you in the centre, and then—now listen to this, for it is very odd—I found that drawing on the chapel floor, and your version and mine were the same."

"You didn't know it was I who had dropped it?"

"No, I didn't know who had dropped it. Not knowing, I felt justified in stealing it."

"Did you know it was a drawing for the east wall?"

"Yes, I guessed that."

"Oh!" groaned Henrietta. "If only we could paint that east wall!

But we couldn't, either of us. We're only water colour artists."

"I tell you what we'll do," said Fra Angelico, nodding towards the big easel. "When I've finished your portrait we'll paint our picture together on this piece of paper ... The picture we'd like to do on the east wall if only we knew how."

"Oh!" cried Henrietta in ecstasy. "May I help?"

"I shall need your help. I'm not quite sure, for instance, why you had to make the Virgin's cloak sweep right round over the manger like that, or why Joseph's arm is raised so high. Isn't it a bit exaggerated? Mind you, this is no carping criticism. It's just a friendly argument between one artist and another."

"Of course," said Henrietta equably. "It has to be like that because the Baby needs looking after. People do need it sometimes."

"Babies," corrected Fra Angelico.

"People," corrected Henrietta. "Grown-ups too. Some grown-ups can be very tiresome and selfish when they won't let themselves be helped. They give a lot of trouble."

"Really," said Fra Angelico. "You speak very feelingly, as though from personal experience."

"Yes," said Henrietta. "I find, myself, that people generally do what I tell them. But my grandfather has had a lot of trouble that way."

Fra Angelico was painting again. "But doesn't your grandfather think people should stand on their own feet?" he asked.

"Yes," said Henrietta. "When they're on them. But often they're not on them, you know. They have to be put there, like tortoises."

"Tortoises?"

"Don't you know about tortoises?" asked Henrietta. "If they get on their backs by accident they can't get on their feet again unless someone picks them up and puts them there. And they let themselves be righted. They're only too pleased. I once had a tortoise."

"What was its name?"

"Charles … Why is Father lending you our step-ladder?"

Fra Angelico started slightly. Busy with his work as he was Henrietta's mind was moving a little too quickly for him. "What step-ladder?" he asked weakly.

"Ours, that Father says you'll need later on. What do you want it for?"

"To get fresh air into my room," said Fra Angelico. "It only has a skylight, and I need a ladder to open it. Would you like to rest a little now and eat a prauleen? And then perhaps we'd better not talk

so much. I find your conversation gives me so much to think about that I can't concentrate on my work."

"I expect you've come unclicked," said Henrietta understandingly. "You'd better rest, too, and have a prauleen. And after that I won't speak, and you can click again."

Nor did she. She sat in a still and lovely silence that was in itself an inspiration to the man who painted her. Only the striking of the Cathedral clock and the rustle of pigeons' wings disturbed their peace; and they were more an accentuation of it than an interruption. He had thought that he would never paint again, but this peace was like a deep well; down at the bottom of it the waters of inspiration sprang up unchanged.

And then Ferranti came back.

"But you've only been gone ten minutes," they complained.

"I've been gone two hours," he said.

Henrietta smiled at him. It had been good of him to leave them two hours.

"May I see the portrait?" he asked.

"Not yet," said Fra Angelico. "I hate my things being looked at while I'm still only feeling after what I want. Criticism, then, only makes one forget what one did want."

"Very well," acquiesced Ferranti.

That was good of him, too, Henrietta thought. But then, of course, he understood. He made things too. She slipped off her chair, put on her coat and cap, said good-bye very politely to Fra Angelico, and went away at once with her father. Henrietta was like that. She knew when things had to stop. She knew that pleasure, to be pleasure, must come to an end.

Chapter VII

The days that followed were wonderful ones for Henrietta, but they went far too quickly. Her portrait was soon done and taken up to London by Ferranti, to be framed for Grandfather's Christmas present. Then they started on the Christmas picture. Henrietta was not allowed to help with the actual drawing of the figures, except with advice, for Fra Angelico had very strong ideas about these figures, and very strange some of them were, Henrietta thought, for he did not make the people look life-like, as he had made her in the portrait, he made them very flat and queer and odd, like the figures in medieval paintings. But yet they *were* alive. They were very much alive. The love of Mary, the protective tenderness of Joseph, the awe and devotion of the shepherds and the animals, and the joy of the angel, were all somehow expressed in their figures, even though their faces were as yet a blur. It was very clever of Fra Angelico to make them like that, Henrietta thought, very clever indeed, for he had no models, except herself and Ferranti, and they, though they stood for him, were not a bit like the odd flat people in the picture … And yet they must have been like, for she distinctly saw her father in one of the shepherds, and the angel, whom Fra Angelico was making a child angel and not the great stupendous creature she had herself pictured, was, she could not help seeing, a bit like her … It was very odd.

But when it came to the painting of the draperies she was allowed to help really properly. Fra Angelico showed her how to mix white with her colours, so as to get the smooth flat surface that he wanted, and how to put on the colour so that there were no hard lines, and how to mix one colour with another so as to get all the variations of deepening shadows. And Eric, the dog on the tomb, whose story she had by now told to Fra Angelico, she painted quite by herself. She sketched him herself in the Cathedral, and then Fra Angelico transferred the sketch (improving it during the process) to the picture, and then she painted it … It was all most tremendously exciting.

But it wasn't quite fair because Fra Angelico got far longer at the picture than she did. Owing to the tyranny of lessons she could only go to the studio for such short periods, at those hours when she was supposed by Grandfather and Grandmother to be out for a walk with her father, while he could work all day and, she was inclined to think, most of the night also. Almost before she had had time to savour the full joy of it the picture was finished, and the next time that she and Ferranti went to the studio Fra Angelico wasn't there.

"He's gone!" cried Henrietta, and a dreadful despair seized her. "Gone for good!"

"Not for good," Ferranti answered her. "Only for a little while. You'll see him and the picture again at Christmas."

But Henrietta was inconsolable until she found a note with "For Henrietta" on it pinned to one of the easels. "Dear Suora Angelico," it said. "I'll be back. Meanwhile please honour me by using my studio, brushes, paints and paper, to complete as many pictures as possible before I see you again. Might I suggest a series of angelic portraits? You, dear Suora Angelico, being so nearly related to the creatures, will doubtless be able to persuade them to come in at the window to sit for you."

"It's nice of him to call me Suora Angelico!" said Henrietta. "Almost as though I was as good an artist as he is."

"I doubt," said Ferranti, "if you'll ever have a nicer compliment from a man or a painter."

Henrietta was pleased, so pleased that she did not grieve any more because Fra Angelico had gone away, but gave herself up joyously to the gift he had given her. Ferranti brought her every day to the studio, and then, with amazing understanding, went away and left her; and she would paint on and on regardless of time, undisturbed by any one except old Martha bringing her lollipops, until he fetched her again. She thought that she had never been so happy; that she never again would be so happy. Here, she thought, was all she would ever ask of life; an empty room under the sky, a sheet of blank paper, a paint brush and a box of paints. This was her kingdom.

By December the twenty-second, which was the date she had decided on for leaving the studio and devoting herself at home to the cross-stitch tea-cosy she was making for Grandmother, she had quite an imposing array of portraits to her credit, all stitched together in a neat book for Grandfather's Christmas present.

She had painted all the angels she had ever heard about; the four archangels, Michael, Gabriel, Raphael and Asrael, superb creatures with huge wings like the feathered golden clouds she could see out of the window when the sun was setting; the warrior angels with their swords in their hands and flame in their eyes; the seraphs with their six wings, purple and blue wings like the shadows that crept across the Market Place when the first stars shone out and the earth veiled her face in awe of them, covering their eyes before the eyes of God; the guardian angels, less well dressed than the others, a little overworked and harassed because their human charges gave them such a lot of trouble, but very lovely all the same; and jolly fat little bodiless cherubs like the carvings in her room.

Ferranti, overwhelmed by these portraits, asked Henrietta if the angels really had come in through the window to sit for her. But Henrietta, a truthful child, said she would not like to say for certain; it was true she had heard the rustling of wings, but it might only have been the pigeons, and though she had seen wonderful colours, and a lot of billowing whiteness, it might only have been the sunset and the great clouds passing by … Anyhow, she said to her father, as he helped her pack up the pictures in an old newspaper she had brought from home for the purpose, she hoped Grandfather would be pleased.

But Ferranti did not answer, for he was staring at the newspaper. "Where did you get this, Gabrielle?" he asked her.

"Out of the cupboard where Ellen puts the old newspapers, ready for when the sweep comes," said Henrietta, peeping over his shoulder. "What an old one," she added, seeing its date. "The day you came home."

Ferranti said no more, but he cut something out of the paper and put it in his pocket. Then they went home; at least Henrietta did, for Ferranti left her at the west door of the Cathedral because there was something or other he wanted to do inside. He was late for lunch, of course, and Henrietta was hard put to it to find excuses for him.

Chapter VIII

The morning of Christmas Eve dawned at last, the most thrilling Christmas Eve that Henrietta had ever known, and with it came the revelation of the secret that Grandfather and Hugh Anthony had been engaged upon. They had been decorating the Christmas tree that Ferranti had brought. Everyone had known that, of course, for Hugh Anthony's conversation had been full of stars and candles for weeks past, and the very inadequate screen of greenery which had been erected before the Christmas tree, standing in the greenhouse, had by no means hidden its glory. But what everybody had not known was that Grandfather had got the Dean's permission to put it in the chapel of Nicolas de Malden for the carol service, which ever since the service of re-dedication had taken place every year at eight o'clock in the evening in the crypt, in honour of St. Nicolas the Christmas saint, and of Nicolas de Malden the painter. They would all take it there, Grandfather announced at breakfast, as soon as they had finished dealing with their eggs and bacon, and he felt in his pocket for his bunch of keys.

But the key of the chapel was not on it and Grandfather's rosy face was puckered with distress. "Now what did I do with that key?" he murmured. "Jane dear, what in the world did I do with that key?"

"I have no idea, Theobald," said Grandmother severely. "In all probability it dropped from your pocket while gardening; you are exceedingly careless. But you can borrow the key from one of the other Canons."

"They've probably mislaid theirs too," sighed Grandfather. "Not one of them goes into the chapel in the winter; only in the summer when they have visitors to show it to. They are amazingly forgetful of its beauty. They wouldn't see it all winter if it wasn't for the carol service. Did I lend the key to anyone?"

Henrietta fixed reproachful eyes upon Ferranti. "Father!" she said, "I told you weeks ago to give it back to Grandfather."

"So you did," said Ferranti.

"But you've got it?" urged Henrietta.

"To tell you the truth," said Ferranti airily, "I haven't. I lent it to a man who went up to London yesterday … But he'll be back by the afternoon train."

"But I want to take down the Christmas tree this morning," said Hugh Anthony, outraged. "I've something else to do this afternoon."

"It's all right," said Ferranti, suddenly remembering something. "He told me he'd leave it under a stone in the crypt. Just for the moment I'd forgotten." And he helped himself to marmalade with the lavishness of a man who considers his conduct to be beyond reproach. The others disagreed with him about his conduct.

Grandmother, pouring herself out another cup of tea, said nothing with a volume of meaning, Grandfather's blue eyes were very sad and Henrietta found herself unable to swallow her last piece of toast … It was naughty of Father not to have given the key back to Grandfather. He had no business to lend it to any one at all, even though she guessed that in this case it was to Fra Angelico, who had doubtless gone up to London to fetch her framed portrait. She was disappointed in him … Hugh Anthony was as undisturbed as Ferranti himself. The key was there, and that was all that mattered. He would now have the afternoon before him in which to perfect a system of booby traps which to-morrow was to operate all over the house as a Christmas present to everybody.

After breakfast Grandfather, Ferranti, Henrietta and Hugh Anthony put on all their warmest clothes, for it was snowing and

137

very cold again, and adjourned to the greenhouse with the wheel-barrow to fetch the Christmas tree. Bates had already gone on to the Cathedral with a large barrow full of potted plants and holly for the Christmas decorations. That glorious decorating! Henrietta gave two delighted skips. When they had taken the Christmas tree to the chapel she would be able to help with it. Advent was over now and festival colour would flood the Cathedral again.

The Christmas tree was superb and Grandfather and Hugh Anthony must have worked like blacks to decorate it. It was covered with little figures of angels and beasts, birds and flowers, cut out of pictures and mounted upon cardboard, and as like as Grandfather and Hugh Anthony could get them to the old missals that Nicolas

de Malden used to paint. There were gold and silver balls, too, and myriads of candles, and a great silver star on the top. Henrietta was almost speechless with admiration and Ferranti, lifting the glittering thing into the wheel-barrow, declared himself to be almost blinded by its glory.

Then they started, Ferranti wheeling the barrow, Grandfather and Henrietta holding the Christmas tree steady, and Hugh Anthony going on ahead doing nothing at all.

"You ought to be doing this instead of me, Hugh Anthony," complained Henrietta.

"Why?" asked Hugh Anthony.

"Because gentlemen always do things instead of ladies."

"Why?" asked Hugh Anthony.

"Because the strong always help the weak," said Grandfather.

"Why?" asked Hugh Anthony.

"Because it is the command of God that they should do so," said Grandfather sternly. "It says so in the Bible. Come along back and hold this tree steady instead of Henrietta."

Hugh Anthony came along back with a sunny smile and did so. His "difficult" moods were mercifully always of short duration, and nothing gave him greater satisfaction than to pursue a question of conduct back to its explanation. Now that he knew why he had to help Henrietta he was willing, and even pleased, to do so.

Ferranti, who had been silent for some time, suddenly spoke.

"Owing to this business of the Christmas tree," he said, "I shall be obliged to let out this morning a secret which I had meant to keep until the carol service."

"Dear me," said Grandfather.

"*The* secret?" asked Henrietta.

"Yes," said Ferranti, "and heaven knows what you'll all say about it."

He spoke so seriously that the others said no more. They

perceived that this was no trivial secret but something rather shattering. Ferranti even seemed anxious about it. Henrietta knew the feeling; terror lest something prepared and brooded over for very long, created to give joy, should after all fail of its intention. She stopped kicking up the snow at the side of the road and ran to walk beside him behind the barrow.

It was a day very like that other day, the day when she had first seen Fra Angelico. There was the same bright crystal sky, the same dazzling snow and cold rarefied air, as though they had been lifted up into some high mountain country. They went in through the west door and there, as always, was the Child, cold and covered with snow, holding out his arms in welcome to the house of life, and, as always, Henrietta wished she could carry him inside, out of the bitter wind.

"Will it be terrible inside to-day?" she asked him wordlessly. "Will it be frightening, like it was the other time?"

But the moment she got inside she knew it was not frightening to-day. It was to-day not so much the house of life as the house of comfort inside life. Warmth and colour seemed to meet her everywhere, people and voices and an indescribable feeling of excited preparation ... Christmas Day to-morrow ... The stoves had been stoked up and the decorating, zealously carried out by all the ladies of the Close, was already well started. The slanting sunbeams lit on holly berries like little scarlet lamps, and laurel wreaths laid upon the tombs of the heroes and tall lilies standing beside the statues of the saints. No one could reach the gilded statue of the Madonna and Child, far up on the great inverted arch, but the sun had seen to it that it lacked no Christmas glory. Golden light enveloped it, streaming from it as though it was a lamp that lit the whole Cathedral. How lovely it was in here to-day, thought Henrietta. How lovely! If only she could pick up armfuls of the warmth and comfort, carry it to the west door and fling it outside across the snow to the figures who toiled out there alone in the cold

… Like that man who weeks ago she had seen as in a vision toiling across a snowy moor and until this moment had quite forgotten … She was suddenly glad that she had not been able to bring the snowy statue of the Child inside with her. She was glad that he was outside with those who were cold and desolate as well as inside with the warm and comforted.

They wheeled the barrow as softly as they could past the decorated chantries and glowing flower-filled chapels, and they had great fun getting it down the steps of the crypt. They found the key of the chapel under a stone in a dark corner, and Ferranti unlocked the door and went in first to light the candles. He wouldn't let the rest of them come in until he had finished lighting them, and then he opened the door wide and said, "Now!" His voice was very quiet and his face was quiet too. He looked like someone listening to a glorious piece of music.

Grandfather went in first and the children followed, and they stood in a row, staring. Then Grandfather groped his way to the bench and sat down rather suddenly. He had gone quite white. Ferranti, looking at him, suddenly reproached himself with violence. He ought to have prepared Grandfather for what he was to see. One was apt to forget, so full of vitality was he, how very old Grandfather really was … But Henrietta was white, too; and Hugh Anthony, for once in his life, was smitten speechless, his eyes and mouth three large o's in his astonished face.

The east wall was finished. Pictured upon it in form so gracious and colour so lovely that they took the breath away, was the First Coming. Here were no judge in splendour, no demons and terrified sinners such as covered the other walls and the roof; only a Child and his Mother, shepherds and gentle beasts. The picture that Henrietta had helped to paint in Fra Angelico's studio from her own drawing was miraculously here upon the wall. But transformed. This picture, beside that, was in comparison as an opened lily to the unfolded bud; and in comparison with Henrietta's drawing it was as the full stature of the plant to the seed from which it springs ... Yet the seed had been hers ... It was the proudest moment of her life. And she wasn't only proud of herself, she was proud of her brother too, he who was also so nearly related to the angels. She stood with her head high and her eyes very bright and shining ... There are moments when it is surely permissible for a human creature to be proud.

Hugh Anthony's inquiring mind was never stunned for long, and it was he who spoke first.

"Why is the Angel Gabriel only a little girl?" he asked.

"Look again and you'll see why," said Ferranti.

"Why!" cried Hugh Anthony, "it's Henrietta!" He paused. "And the young shepherd is you, and St. Joseph is Grandfather." He paused again. "I'm not there!" he added with a certain outrage.

Henrietta slipped her hand into his. "How could you be?" she murmured consolingly. "Fra Angelico has never seen you." And then she stopped, for it occurred to her that Fra Angelico had never seen Grandfather either; and yet there was Grandfather, in all his round and comfortable benignity, as large as life upon the wall.

"Who's Fra Angelico?" continued Hugh Anthony.

"The man who painted that picture."

"Oh," said Hugh Anthony. "What will the Dean say at all this going on without his knowing?"

This was an aspect of the affair that had not hitherto occurred to Ferranti. "I think it will be all right," he said a little uneasily. "He's short sighted; he'll not recognize the portraits. I think it'll be all right."

"Of course it will be all right," said Grandfather in a voice of thunder, suddenly coming to. "Any man who did not rejoice in that superb fresco would be a fool ... And it was, of course, in the original agreement that that wall as well as the others should be restored." He got up and came to Ferranti, gripping his arm as in a vice. "Where's Nicolas?" he demanded sternly, shaking the arm a little. "What in the name of heaven have you done with Nicolas?"

"He's up in London," said Ferranti. "But he'll be back to-night. He saw an advertisement in an old newspaper that concerned him. Good luck for him, we thought. He's gone up to see about it."

"Ah!" said Grandfather, letting out his breath in a deep sigh; but he did not ask what the advertisement was. "But why in the world did he not come to me?" he demanded, and Henrietta thought there was anguish in his tone. "Why did he not come to me?"

"Pride," said Ferranti. "You've no idea of the trouble I've had with him. He has an appalling pride." He looked round. "The pride of one of those devils of his upon the wall ... Come outside and I'll tell you."

He drew Grandfather outside into the crypt, Hugh Anthony, all ears, scuttling after. Henrietta was left alone in the chapel, and now it was her turn to sit down rather hurriedly upon the seat.

So Fra Angelico was the second Nicolas. Why had she not realized that? How incredibly stupid one could be at eleven years old!

"But pride is good sometimes," she said to herself, remembering that fine thrill of it that had gone through her when she first saw the fresco. "Good sometimes and bad sometimes."

Then she looked attentively at the fresco, to see if Nicolas had stressed in this picture, as she had made him do in the other one, humanity's need of mutual help. Yes, he had. The virgin's cloak sheltered the manger and Grandfather's—no, Joseph's—arm was raised high in protection. The Baby, so guarded, looked very tiny and peacefully submissive in the flowering hay. But his eyes were wide open and aware. Henrietta could see that his acceptance was not for long. Soon he would be outside in the cold; giving a great deal more than ever he had been given ... What a lot could be said with a paint brush. What a lot Nicolas had said, and, at last, understood.

Chapter IX

The rest of the morning Henrietta and Hugh Anthony spent in settling the Christmas tree in the chapel, and the afternoon was filled up with a great deal of private activity in dark corners, but after tea, their own affairs disposed of, they helped Grandfather and Ferranti to put lighted candles in all the window panes to welcome the Christ Child. This lovely old custom was disapproved of by Grandmother, who said the grease dripped. But she was too kind-hearted to stop their pleasure. She only said firmly that lovely old custom, or no lovely old custom, she would not have that mess in the drawing-room; and retired thither with a tolerant smile to enjoy her knitting in peace and quiet, leaving them to do what they liked with the rest of the house.

They were just sticking the last candles on the ledges of the study window when they heard the front door bang, and quick steps across the hall. The room was dim, lit only by the fire, the candles being yet unlighted, but even so Henrietta had no difficulty in recognizing the tall slim figure standing in the doorway ... It was standing in the doorway, hesitating to come in, that she had seen him first ... She took a flying leap from the window-sill and landed beside him.

He pulled one of her pig-tails affectionately, but took no further notice of her. He went straight to Grandfather.

"I suppose someone left you a legacy?" he said gently. "Out of your own pocket, surely, you could not have spared so much?"

"Yes," said Grandfather. "It was a legacy I do not need."

"The moment I got in that office," said Nicolas, "the moment they told me of that sum of money paid to my account to put me on my feet again, I knew whom it had come from. Only you would have done it."

"You'll take it?" asked Grandfather anxiously. "You'll take it?"

Nicolas stiffened. Even now Henrietta could feel that yielding did not come easily. "I'll take it," he said at last, harshly and with difficulty. "And thank you."

His whole figure relaxed, as though in relief from strain. The difficult moment over he turned thankfully to Henrietta and pulled her other pig-tail. "The portrait," he told Ferranti, "is in the hall."

The rest of the evening seemed to Henrietta to pass in a blissful dream. Grandfather's delight over Nicolas's portrait of her, and her portraits of the angels, which he really should not have been given until the morning, only she could not wait to give them to him, lasted until supper; and then came Nicolas's introduction to Grandmother, and the breaking to her very gently that he was staying the night, was in fact staying several nights, which passed off a good deal better than any one had dared to hope, Grandmother having just turned the heel of her sock successfully and being in an exceptionally good mood. Then came the early supper, sausage-rolls and jelly, much enjoyed, and then they all started for the carol service in the crypt.

Even Grandmother, well wrapped up, came to this, and walked to the Cathedral leaning most graciously upon Ferranti's arm, and so melted by the festive season that she chatted to him with a warmth of affection that nearly knocked him over backwards. Hugh Anthony, walking on her other side, carrying her hymn-book and spectacles, was so astonished that the word "why" never passed his lips once, all the way from the Close to the west door of the Cathedral, when he suddenly remarked, "Why does Christmas come only once a year? I think it's a great mistake that it doesn't come oftener."

Henrietta walked behind between Grandfather and Nicolas, so

lost in her happy dreams that she only attended very vaguely to what they were saying over her head.

"What have you been doing, Nicolas, all this last year?" Grandfather was asking.

"Tramping. Picking up what work I could. A bad time … It's past."

"And now you're happy?" asked Grandfather anxiously.

"Yes. I have been judged. I've paid. It's over. Odd, wasn't it, that the last picture I painted before—the mess, was the Judgment Day, and the first one afterwards the Christmas story?"

"Not at all odd," said Grandfather. "Merely the natural sequence of events. After judgment rebirth."

"A few months ago," said Nicolas, "I thought Nicolas Broadbent the painter was dead, leaving John Barnes the convict to drag on as best he could. But now it seems it's the other way round. In that studio above the Market Place it was John Barnes who died, and Nicolas who came alive again."

"It is Nicolas who is the real man, I think," said Grandfather. "Here we are. I must leave you and go to the vestry. I shall have to break it to them in the vestry before we go down. Dear me, I hope we shall have no trouble with the Dean. Now that the moment is upon me I am a little nervous."

Only the clergy were actually inside the chapel during the annual carol service, for there was no room for anyone else. The rest of the congregation were in the crypt, but after the service they all filed into the chapel to think a little while of Santa Claus and Nicolas de Malden; and some few of them perhaps of Nicolas Broadbent.

What with one thing and another Grandmother and her party had been long over supper and were a little late in getting to the Cathedral; the crypt was already full of people. Almost the whole of Torminster was gathered there, row after row of them reaching away into the shadows, those deep velvety underground shadows whose mystery the lighted candles in tall iron sconces could not conquer, only intensify. They knew nothing yet, of course, but their eyes were fixed upon the open door of the brightly lighted chapel, from which the light was streaming out even more brilliantly than usual … Peppercorn, the verger, who had been let into the secret and was most excited about it, must have lit every one of the Christmas tree candles, as well as the altar ones, Henrietta thought … The chapel was the focal point of their joy to-night; it was for the time being the heart of the whole great darkened Cathedral.

But Peppercorn had kept places for them, and showed them into them with much bustling ostentation. "You'll get a good view from here," he whispered hoarsely. "You'll see the faces of the reverend gentlemen when it dawns upon them, like. A fair treat it will be."

"Thank you, Peppercorn," said Grandmother with rather crushing dignity, and he hurried away, for it was his part to lead the clergy down from the vestry, his wand of office held aloft, robed in the sombre dignity of his long black gown that seemed to hold in its whispering folds the ghosts of a hundred dead and gone processions … Henrietta was glad it was so dark in the crypt; especially so in the corner where they were sitting. It made it so much easier for Nicolas that no one could recognize him.

Eight o'clock struck, the deep notes of it falling down and down from the heights of the starry sky to this deep vault where they were sitting. Then there was an utter silence, not a sound from the waiting congregation, not even the rustle of a turning page or the breath of a sigh, nothing but a deep silence in which, surely, the happy ghosts were gathering thickly in the shadows. Henrietta could picture them; the cowled monks who had served the monastery, the townspeople who had made the city of Torminster, all the men and women and little children who had lived out their lives in the shelter of the great Cathedral and welcomed Christmas year after year, generation after generation, in this very place; and Nicolas de Malden himself, clad in his dark brown habit, girt about the waist with rope, not gaunt and dying as when he had painted the chapel walls but happy and enthralled as she had so often seen him working at his missal.

The silence was broken by a thin thread of music. Far away in the nave the choir were singing.

> *Oh little town of Bethlehem,*
> *How still we see thee lie!*
> *Above thy deep and dreamless sleep*
> *The silent stars go by.*
> *Yet in thy dark streets shineth*
> *The everlasting light;*
> *The hopes and fears of all the years*
> *Are met in thee to-night.*

Their voices swelled and grew louder, for they had reached the entrance to the crypt and were coming slowly down the worn steps; so worn by countless worshippers that they were bent to the shape of a bow as though always weighed down by the feet of the multitude.

> *Oh morning stars, together*
> *Proclaim the holy birth.*
> *And praises sing to God the king,*
> *And peace to men on earth;*
> *For Christ is born of Mary;*
> *And, gathered all above,*
> *While mortals sleep, the angels keep*
> *Their watch of wondering love.*

The congregation could sing too now, as the Cross bearer came into sight with behind him the choir in their red festival cassocks, and then Peppercorn leading the clergy.

> *How silently, how silently,*
> *The wondrous gift is given!*
> *So God imparts to human hearts*
> *The blessings of his heaven.*

148

No ear may hear his coming;
But in this world of sin,
When meek souls will receive him, still
The dear Christ enters in.

The clergy were all in the chapel now, and Henrietta could see their faces through the open door. It was funny and yet it was touching. Shock, incredulity, bewilderment and wonder took possession of their faces one by one, to be followed at last by that look of adoration and peace that had been on Grandfather's face from the beginning; that peace which only the experience of perfection can give to a human soul. The Dean, a gentleman of uncertain temper, looked as peaceful as any. They need not have feared him.

They sang all the familiar carols one by one in the echoing darkness, and then the Dean, standing in the chapel door, blessed them, and the clergy and choir went away as they had come, singing up the steps and down the nave, their voices dying away into a thread of sound and then to silence. Then the congregation came to life and began to move towards the chapel for their annual sight of those superb painted walls. Grandmother, Ferranti and Hugh Anthony went with them, eager to hear what they said when they saw the missal-like Christmas tree, the Baby and the shepherds.

But Nicolas and Henrietta fled up the steps to the deserted nave above, overwhelmed by the terror which seizes all creators when their creation is exposed for the first time to the gaze of man ... The first Creator felt it, surely, when Adam's eyes opened upon the garden which he had made ... But it was a happy terror and they laughed as they held hands in the darkness; for they had looked upon what they had made and they knew that it was very good.

Nine o'clock struck and, as always at the conclusion of the carol service, the Christmas bells began to ring.